'I...I don't understand.' Kate stared at him.

'I asked for a doctor, not a kindergarten teacher. Obviously I didn't make my requirements clear enough.'

'I can assure you I'm fully qualified. I did my training at St Maud's where for the past year I was a registrar...'

'I don't need a list of your qualifications,' Sam Brady replied harshly. 'I don't doubt that on paper they look good but, believe me, you won't last out here any longer than the others.'

GW01066324

Jean Evans was born in Leicester and married shortly before her seventeenth birthday. She has two married daughters and several grandchildren. She gains valuable information and background for her medical romances from her husband, who is a senior nursing administrator. She now lives in Hampshire, close to the New Forest, and within easy reach of the historic city of Winchester.

Recent titles by the same author:

A PRACTICE MADE PERFECT
HEART ON THE LINE
THE FRAGILE HEART

TAKE A CHANCE ON LOVE

BY
JEAN EVANS

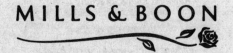

MILLS & BOON

DID YOU PURCHASE THIS BOOK WITHOUT A COVER?
If you did, you should be aware it is **stolen property** as it was
reported *unsold and destroyed* by a retailer. Neither the Author
nor the publisher has received any payment for this book.

*All the characters in this book have no existence outside the imagina-
tion of the author, and have no relation whatsoever to anyone bearing
the same name or names. They are not even distantly inspired by any
individual known or unknown to the author, and all the incidents are
pure invention.*

*All Rights Reserved including the right of reproduction in whole or
in part in any form. This edition is published by arrangement with
Harlequin Enterprises II B.V. The text of this publication or any part
thereof may not be reproduced or transmitted in any form or by any
means, electronic or mechanical, including photocopying, recording,
storage in an information retrieval system, or otherwise, without the
written permission of the publisher.*

*This book is sold subject to the condition that it shall not, by way of
trade or otherwise, be lent, resold, hired out or otherwise circulated
without the prior consent of the publisher in any form of binding or
cover other than that in which it is published and without a similar
condition including this condition being imposed on the subsequent
purchaser.*

*MILLS & BOON and MILLS & BOON with the Rose Device
are registered trademarks of the publisher.*

*First published in Great Britain 1997
Harlequin Mills & Boon Limited,
Eton House, 18-24 Paradise Road, Richmond, Surrey TW9 1SR*

© Jean Evans 1997

ISBN 0 263 80000 8

*Set in Times 10 on 11 pt. by
Rowland Phototypesetting Limited
Bury St Edmunds, Suffolk*

03-9701-50637-D

*Printed and bound in Great Britain
by Mackays of Chatham PLC, Chatham*

CHAPTER ONE

'I'M SERIOUSLY beginning to think I'm getting too old for this sort of thing.' Dr David Stewart wearily dropped his briefcase and coat onto a chair before sniffing the air appreciatively. 'Mmm, something smells good.'

'Casserole. I made it last night so it just needed popping in the oven.' Kate Stewart poured a mug of coffee, her lips twitching with amusement. For all that her father kept threatening to retire, she knew that he loved his work; that his life revolved around the Derbyshire practice—especially since her mother had died five years ago. 'Here, drink this—it will warm you up.' She handed him the mug. 'I take it it was a busy surgery?'

He brushed a few drops of sleet from his hair, chafing his hands before hunting for his pipe. 'This wretched flu epidemic seems to be hanging on. Most of our patients would be better off taking a couple of aspirins and staying indoors, but it's the old folk I worry about— the ones who can't get out and about. They're the vulnerable ones.'

'I know what you mean.' Frowning, Kate tested the vegetables and reached for the plates. 'We've had several cases of pneumonia admitted to the hospital in the past week. If things go on at this rate there could be a shortage of beds. Still—' she gave a slight smile '—a few days more and that won't be my problem, and after a day like today I'm actually beginning to feel quite relieved.'

'Bad, was it?'

'Mmm, sort of.' She placed the casserole dish on the table. 'A kiddy—two-year-old with a Wilms' tumour.'

David Stewart drew in a breath. 'Poor little devil.'

5

'I know.' Kate frowned. 'It's the parents I feel sorry for. They've had a rough time since they first discovered the lump a few weeks ago. Since then everything's happened in a bit of a rush.'

'How is he doing?'

She smiled. 'Actually he's doing quite nicely. He went down for surgery today. You know, I'm almost ashamed to admit it but it's the first Wilms' I've seen.'

'Not surprising, really; they're quite rare, thank God. Mind you, his chances should be pretty good now that the kidney's been removed.'

Kate nodded, tucking a strand of chestnut-coloured hair behind her ear. 'I was amazed to see how large the tumour was. The good thing is that it was completely encapsulated so it came away cleanly. None of the other major organs was involved, thank heavens.'

'The parents must be relieved.'

'Over the moon. Of course the little chap isn't entirely out of the woods yet. They're still waiting for the results of the biopsy but. . .' she grinned, moving to sit at the table '. . .it's looking good, so at least I shall be leaving on a happy note.'

Helping himself to potatoes, David Stewart studied his daughter and experienced a familiar surge of pride even as he noted the fine shadows beneath her grey-blue eyes. 'You're going to miss it, aren't you?'

'Probably.' Kate busied herself, serving out the casserole, glad of an excuse to avoid his gaze and wishing that she could escape this particular conversation. They had had it too many times over the past few months and she knew precisely where it was leading. She ladled carrots onto her plate.

'I suppose it's bound to seem strange at first—after all, I trained at St Maud's. Sometimes I feel as if I've been there for ever. I've certainly made a lot of friends.' Her smiled faded. 'I shall miss them, yes, but that doesn't mean I'm not looking forward to a new challenge.'

'I still don't see why it had to be Africa,' her father protested. 'I know things didn't work out between you and young Carter. How he has the gall to stay around here—even worse, in the same hospital—is beyond me.' He glanced up at her. 'I do still have some influence, you know—people on various committees. If you wanted, I'm sure I could apply some pressure and get him eased out. That girlfriend of his, too.'

Neither of them was smiling now. Kate pushed her barely touched plate away, refusing to meet his gaze and let him see that he was in danger of touching upon what was still a very raw nerve.

'We've been through all this, Dad. Jeremy has every right to stay in Bedensfield. I know you don't like him but he's a damn good doctor and St Maud's is lucky to have him. Why should he move, give it all up, just because. . .?' She swallowed hard. 'Just because he fell in love with someone else? It's hardly Anna's fault. I know her. I *like* her. She's a good doctor too. Besides, it isn't as if Jeremy deceived me in any way.'

'Typical!' David Stewart glared at her from under his beetling, greying brow. 'I might have known you'd see everyone else's point of view.'

'Oh, Dad. What use are recriminations? It's done. Jeremy fell in love with someone else—it's as simple as that. He would hardly have been doing me a favour in keeping up a pretence. In any case, it's not as if we were officially engaged.'

'But everyone assumed that's where it was leading,' her father growled. 'I don't know how you can bear to see him and that girl together.'

'I don't actually see too much of them, as it happens,' Kate assured him. 'Anyway, it's not for much longer and I'd really rather not discuss it, Dad. It's not important.'

He shot her a cynical look. 'That's why you're off to Africa, is it?'

Stifling a sigh, she pushed her chair back and gave him a hug. 'It's not the end of the world, you know.'

He grunted. 'No, just the other side. Couldn't you have picked somewhere closer to home?' His eyes were suspiciously bright. Reaching for a handkerchief, he blew his nose hard. 'Why not Birmingham? There's nothing wrong with Birmingham. It's a nice place.'

'I know it is.' She moved to stand behind him, her arms round his shoulders as she kissed the top of his head. 'But I needed a new challenge. I feel I can do something really worthwhile in Africa and it's not as if it's a sudden whim. You know Jeremy and I. . . You know I've been thinking about it for some time. They need doctors, Dad. Besides, my initial contract is only for three months.'

He grunted, knowing when he was beaten. 'And what about this Brody chap? What do you know about him?'

'*Brady*, Dad; it's Dr Brady, and not a lot.' She smiled indulgently, recognising his concerns. 'He couldn't be in London when I went for my interview, but I'll find out soon enough.'

'Yes, well, you'd better take care, that's all.' He sniffed hard. 'And I shall expect at least one letter a week.'

'You'll have it,' she promised, grateful to have the subject of Jeremy closed. She knew that he meant well and was only concerned for her, but her feelings for Jeremy were something that she would have to deal with in her own way. At least in Africa she wouldn't have to see him and Anna every day and time was supposed to be a great healer. She could only hope that it was true.

It was a relief, in the following days, not to have time to dwell on it. There was certainly no let-up at the hospital so that her final day, when at last it dawned, was as hectic as ever—hardly leaving time for good-byes—and in a way she was glad.

It was difficult to believe, as she walked into the staff-room for the last time, that a month from now she would be in Africa, working in a strange environment amongst people she didn't know. It would be like bringing down the final shutter between herself and Jeremy, but that didn't mean that the hurting would stop.

'Some people have all the luck.' Beth Read, who had gone through all the trauma of medical school with Kate, toasted her impending departure with a hastily snatched cup of coffee. Her eyes were misty as she gave Kate a hug. 'Damn it, I was hoping not to make a complete fool of myself. You take good care of yourself, you hear? Now I'm going. Some of us still have to work around here.' Giving her a final hug, she fled, sniffing loudly.

Charlie McLean, the senior casualty officer, grinned as he shook her hand. 'Don't forget to write and tell us how much better off we are.'

Mike Tucker's eyes twinkled as he held her close and kissed her firmly on the mouth. 'In spite of what everyone says, you'll be missed.'

'I'm sure Kate knows that.' Jeremy came in too, his eyes on her flushed face, and she felt herself stiffen. She had hoped that he would make it easier for her by staying away; save her this last painful reminder. But, then, he had no idea of the quiet hell she was still going through.

It needed a real effort of will to smile as he came towards her; to pretend that she wasn't actually hurting like hell when what she really wanted was to rush into his arms and have him tell her not to go; that it had all been a terrible mistake and that he still loved her. She drew in a ragged breath, knowing that it wasn't going to happen.

'I just thought I'd pop in to wish you luck.' He looked

down at her, his face serious. He was tall and fair haired, with a kind of boyish charm that had won her to him instantly.

'Well, I hope I'm not going to need it.' She gave a slight laugh but he didn't respond.

'Africa's a big place. It's a long way from home.' He took her hand in his, looking down at her beautiful face, his expression serious. 'It's funny but I'm only just beginning to realise it's actually going to happen—that I shall still be here and you won't. It seems strange, especially as we talked about going out there together.'

She forced a smile. 'Yes, well, plans can change.'

'I'm serious, Kate. I shall miss you—you do know that?'

She gave a slight laugh. 'The way things are around here I doubt if you'll even have time to notice I'm gone.'

'That's not true.' His expression took on a hint of peevishness. 'I'm hardly likely to be flavour of the month around here when you've gone. I suppose you do realise they'll blame me for your leaving—after what happened?'

She wondered with a brief feeling of resentment how he would react if she said that she understood their feelings then brushed the thought aside, telling herself that she was being ridiculous.

'I'm sure you're wrong,' she managed lightly. 'It was no one's fault. I don't blame you and surely that's what counts?'

He smiled and visibly seemed to relax. 'I'm glad we're still friends. We are, aren't we, Kate?' He reached up a hand to brush a strand of hair from her cheek.

Instinctively she stiffened, catching at his hand. 'Don't, Jeremy, please. This isn't a good idea.' She gathered her bleeper, refusing to see the pained expression in his eyes. If she didn't get out of here soon she was going to make a complete fool of herself. 'I have to go. I hope everything goes well for you. Give my regards to Anna. I'm sure you'll both be very happy.' She headed for the door.

'Kate, wait. Don't go like this. Can't we at least talk?'

'Jeremy.' Anna appeared in the open doorway. She was petite and pretty, her gamine features framed by stylishly bobbed hair. 'I've been looking everywhere for you. I wondered if you'd take a look at Mr Fenwick on Men's Medical for me. I'm not too happy about him.' She smiled at Kate.

'Hi, I was hoping I'd catch you. I wanted to wish you well. We both do, don't we, Jeremy?' She looked up at him and he smiled, his hand resting on her shoulder.

'Yes, of course. That's just what I was saying.'

Kate fled. Jeremy was a part of her life that was over. It had to be, and the sooner she accepted that and made a fresh start the better.

A month later she was on a plane bound for the other side of the world. As they climbed higher and higher through the clouds, gradually leaving behind a mizzly, grey, English day, Kate rested her head back against the seat, closing her eyes and trying to relax. It wasn't easy.

At any other time she would have enjoyed the flight and all the preparations leading up to it, but for some reason this time was different. She felt tired and uncertain about what lay ahead. Africa was light years away from everything she was used to. She would be working with strangers in an environment which, until now, she had only read about or seen on TV.

Without any sense of false modesty, she knew that she was a good doctor but her only experience had been in an English hospital or in her father's rural country practice.

She had been warned at her interview that conditions would be very different at Ramindi. What if she was making the biggest mistake of her life? She fought against a rising sense of panic. It was too late now for regrets. Besides, what was there for her to go back to?

It was galling, as the hours passed, to see most of the other passengers gradually starting to relax and enjoy the in-flight meals or settling back to doze or enjoy a movie. Even though she was exhausted, she finally gave up her own determined attempt to sleep. Her mind seemed to be whirling in all directions, with the result that her skin was pale and she had a niggling headache.

A smiling steward settled a tray of pre-packed food in front of her. It looked fresh and appetising and Kate felt her stomach rumble but, when it came to it, she couldn't bring herself to eat.

Someone would be at the airport to meet her on her arrival—she knew that from the paperwork which had been included with her contract and tickets. She only hoped that whoever it was would have a friendly face and would have booked her into a hotel so that she could at least try to get a decent night's sleep before going on to Ramindi to meet her new employer.

It would be good to settle into a routine again—into the kind of normality that seemed to have been lacking in her life since the day Jeremy had chosen to tell her that he had met someone else. She could still remember her sense of shock. How could she not have seen what was happening? What could she have done differently? Would it have made any difference?

Closing her eyes briefly, Kate wished them well. The pity was that she still loved him. But that was her secret. No one else must ever know.

She turned her head restlessly against the seat, opening her eyes to find her fellow passenger in the adjoining seat looking down at her. Having finished his meal, the man, who had cheerfully introduced himself as Harry Gardener, reached for his gin and tonic and smiled.

'Flying's great, if you happen to like that kind of

thing. Personally, I always find that one or six of these helps.'

She smiled ruefully. 'Right now I'm not so sure that would be a good idea.'

'Holiday, is it?'

'No, actually I'm flying out to start a new job. I'm a doctor.'

'Hey, I'm impressed.' The sixtyish American grinned. 'They certainly make 'em in all shapes and sizes these days. I approve. Better than the crusty old goat I get to see back home.'

Kate laughed. 'I'm joining a medical team based at Ramindi. I don't suppose you know it?'

'Well, now, as it happens I do. Well, not know it exactly but I've heard of it.'

Kate shot him a look. 'You're not. . .?'

'Hell no,' Harry Gardener laughed. 'I leave the doctoring to the rest. I'm just a tin-rattler.'

'Tin-rattler?'

He chuckled. 'Well, sort of. I work for one of the charity organisations—you may have heard of it. Project Overland?'

'Oh, yes. They do some wonderful work.'

'Well, I'm out here to attend an international conference next week. Before that I have to fit in a few visits. I suppose you could say it's a fact-finding tour.' He smiled wryly. 'Resources are always finite. There are so many worthwhile causes. It's never an easy task, allocating funds. There are always going to be losers. But I do know about Ramindi, as it happens. They're doing a great job.'

Kate smiled. 'I've heard a lot about it but the closer I get the more nervous I feel.'

'It's a good project. I was in at the beginning, so to speak. The organisation helped to raise funds. Of course, I worked mostly with George at the time.'

'George?'

'George Reynolds. He took over as chief medical officer when the hospital first opened.'

Kate frowned. 'But I thought Dr Brady was in charge.'

'Oh, Sam came on the scene later, as George's deputy, so we didn't actually get to meet. But from what I've heard he's damn good at his job.'

Harry drained his drink and looked hopefully for the stewardess. 'I heard Sam did a spell in the States and before that in one of your teaching hospitals.'

He was probably quite old, then, Kate thought, busily slotting pieces of the mental picture she had been trying to build of her new boss into place. Probably nearing retirement and serving out his time before returning to England.

Harry tilted his glass. 'You should try one of these. Good for the nerves.'

Kate smiled at the stewardess and ordered coffee, to Harry's obvious disapproval.

'Coffee'll keep you awake.'

But there wasn't much chance that she would sleep anyway, not with so much going on inside her head. Kate smiled, turning to gaze out of the window into the cloudless heat of a brilliant day.

The sea stretched below, a vivid, shimmering expanse of silver-blue reaching out to lap against the distant coastline, and Kate felt her pulse rate quicken. It was all like part of some incredible dream and only the small knot of tension in her stomach reminded her that it was very much for real.

She stared at her reflection in the window, briefly raking a hand through the swathe of her long, chestnut-coloured hair. Even tied back as it now was, the weight of it seemed to be making her head ache. Or was it nervous tension?

Her thickly lashed grey eyes clouded slightly. It had been a big step—giving up a job she liked and saying goodbye to friends to fly half way round the world to work in a place she didn't know with people she had never met. What would they be like?

Determinedly she closed her eyes, the soft but persistent drumming of the engines adding to the throbbing in her head. A few more hours and she would be in a hotel. The first thing she promised herself was a long, cool shower, followed by at least eight hours of solid, uninterrupted sleep. After that she would be ready for anything.

Some time later Harry Gardener's voice brought her out of an uneasy sleep. 'I think we're coming in to land.'

The plane banked sharply and, with a tremor of excitement, Kate braced herself until, minutes later, it touched down. There was a slight jolt and it was over but for some reason her heart was still beating uncomfortably fast. Swallowing hard on the dryness in her mouth, she gathered her small bag and began to move with the rest of the passengers towards the doors, stepping out into the shimmering heat of an African day.

There was something fascinating about airports, Kate decided as, with Harry beside her, they followed the crowd towards the modern, airy lounge. In here it was cool, though she guessed that outside the temperature was probably in excess of ninety degrees, and she was glad she had decided to wear a lightweight skirt with a pastel-coloured shirt.

All around her people of varying nationalities came and went. New arrivals mingling with those about to leave. She searched the sea of faces then smilingly reminded herself that it was ridiculous trying to look for someone she didn't even know.

Her stomach rumbled suddenly and her legs felt oddly shaky. Jet lag, combined with hunger, was having a strange effect on her nervous system. By now most of the passengers had begun to disperse and as the lounge became almost deserted she looked at her watch, beginning to feel vaguely worried.

'It looks as if we've both been deserted.' Grinning, Harry glanced at his own watch. 'You're sure they said they'd meet you at the airport?'

'Yes, I checked.' Pulling a wry face, she reached for her shoulder-bag. 'Better check again, I suppose.' She frowned. 'What about your driver?'

'Hell, I'm used to this. It's almost routine. At least it makes a change, having someone to wait with. If the worst comes to the worst we can always do some phoning around.'

Kate frowned and re-checked her watch. 'I'll give it a few minutes more. Someone may still turn up.'

'Perhaps I can help?' The distinctly husky male tones coming from behind her made her jump and, turning slowly, Kate found herself staring into a pair of inky blue eyes. The breath momentarily caught in her throat. It was the shock, she told herself, of being accosted by a total stranger.

Slowly she exhaled, brushing a wayward wisp of hair from her forehead as she stared at the man. His face was strong, ruggedly chiselled. His hair was dark, almost black, matching the growth of designer stubble on his chin. He looked as if he'd had a rough night and then some, she decided.

Even so, it was a face which sent an unexpected shock wave running through her. Kate frowned. Not classically good-looking, yet there was something compelling about the tanned features. Not exactly your average vagrant but, then, they probably came in all shapes and sizes, she thought, clutching her bag protectively against her chest.

'I don't think so, thank you.' Her tone was deliberately dismissive, then she felt her colour deepen beneath a disturbingly intense appraisal before he turned to look at Harry.

'Dr Stewart?' He held out a large hand. 'I'm sorry I wasn't here to meet you. I'm Dr Brady, Sam Brady. Welcome to Africa, even it is a little belated.'

Kate found herself listening, the colour flooding into her cheeks as a growing realisation slowly began to dawn.

Taking a deep, controlled breath, she swallowed hard and held out her hand. 'Actually. . .*I'm* Dr Stewart.'

His hand fell as he stood stock-still, a look of disbelief on his face. 'You!'

She stood transfixed, feeling her colour deepen beneath a disturbingly intense appraisal which left her feeling ridiculously shaky, the ageing, fatherly figure of her imaginings swept away in one fell swoop.

It was as if an electric current passed through her. It wasn't just the overwhelming sense of power that seemed to emanate from him as he stood there, it was the look of barely suppressed hostility in the blue eyes that took her breath away—even though she could think of nothing she had done to deserve it.

She was immediately conscious of every line of the taut, muscular body, from his shoulders beneath the open-necked shirt to a slim waist and lean thighs beneath the faded jeans he was wearing. With an effort of will she dragged her gaze up to meet his.

'Guilty, I'm afraid.' Her teeth grated on a smile. 'I'm sorry to be late; the flight was delayed. . .'

Her outstretched hand was ignored as Sam Brady's mouth tightened ominously. 'I take it this is someone's idea of a joke. Either that or someone has mixed up the paperwork.'

She stared at him, feeling the first stirrings of real panic. 'I. . .I don't understand. I was told you asked for. . .'

'I asked for a doctor, not a kindergarten teacher. Obviously I didn't make my requirements clear enough.'

Kate felt her colour deepen as he seemed to take in every detail of her slender figure and delicate features. She was vaguely aware of Harry Gardener reaching for his bag.

'Yes, well, I've just spotted my driver so I'll be on my way.' He squeezed her arm, shooting her a quick look of sympathy. 'Best of luck.' Then he was heading for the exit, leaving Kate to draw a deep breath as she faced the man standing in front of her.

'I *am* a doctor, and I can assure you I'm fully qualified. I did my training at St Maud's where for the past year I was a registrar. . .'

'I don't need a list of your qualifications,' Sam Brady rasped harshly. 'I don't doubt that on paper they look good but I've seen it all before and, believe me, Dr Stewart, you won't last out here any longer than the others.'

CHAPTER TWO

KATE's head jerked up. 'Others?'

'You don't imagine you're the first?' The arrogant mouth twisted. 'It's one thing to get all fired up with missionary zeal in some bright, shiny, modern hospital, Dr Stewart. Unfortunately the reality is here and I can promise you it's like nothing you've ever dared to imagine.'

She swallowed hard. 'I don't think you're being fair. . .'

'I'm being honest. The truth may not be what you want to hear. Well, that's tough. Africa is hot and sweaty. People starve, people die—and I wonder what the hell makes you think you can make a difference?' Sam's frowning gaze swept over her and there was a glint in the blue eyes that might have been intimidating if she hadn't been so angry.

She faced him, breathing hard. 'I didn't come here expecting to change the world overnight. I came to do a job, any job, to the best of my ability because, somehow, foolishly—I see that now—I had the crazy idea that help was needed. I didn't expect to have to face a totally unwarranted assassination of my character and qualifications. Isn't it usual at least to give someone a hearing before passing judgement, Dr Brady?'

She paused for breath and his laser-blue eyes narrowed, sending tiny ripples of shock running through her as she took in the dark eyebrows, a strong nose and firmly sculpted mouth. Sam Brady, she realised, was not a day over thirty-five but he had an aura of toughness. His authority was tangible, underlined in the firm

19

angle of his jaw and the shrewd intelligence lurking behind those blue eyes.

She blinked hard, realising that she was staring. Not only that, but he was returning her stare, measure for measure, and she felt her colour deepen as the coolly brooding gaze subjected her to a flagrantly masculine appraisal that took her breath away.

He raised a hand in mock protest. 'All right, I take back what I said about the kindergarten teacher. As a matter of interest, just how old are you, anyway, Dr Stewart? Twenty-one? Twenty-two?'

'I'm twenty-eight, and kindly don't change the subject.'

His left eyebrow rose mockingly. 'As old as that? And I dare say you've managed to acquire a few personal commitments along the way?'

Kate stared at him, telling herself that she must have misheard, then gasped as his hand suddenly closed over her arm, drawing her close so that her body made contact with the solid wall of his chest. For a few seconds she was stunned by the power of the sensations that ran through her. The breath momentarily snagged in her throat as she tried to free herself, only to feel his grasp tighten. 'H-how dare you? Let me go this instant.'

'Look out!'

Twisting her head, she saw the oncoming baggage trolley gliding past and saw the glint of laughter in his eyes. Then she struggled furiously to break free.

'You were saying?' he drawled softly.

She drew herself up. 'On the contrary, *you* were saying. As far as I'm concerned, Dr Brady, my private life is just that—strictly private. What makes you think you have the right. . .?'

She broke off as his hand suddenly came beneath her elbow, propelling her towards the exit. 'Because I'm responsible for what happens out here,' he said evenly, guiding her round a group of tourists. 'Because you might as well know from the start that I demand one hundred per cent from every member of the team.'

Freeing herself from his grasp, she turned to face him, breathing hard. 'And you don't think I'm up to it, is that it? Because I'm a woman?' She gave a short laugh. 'Isn't your attitude just a little old-fashioned, Dr Brady?'

'My attitude, as you put it, has nothing to do with it. We're a long way from home. If things go wrong we only have ourselves and our collective experience and skills to call upon. No one works in isolation out here, Dr Stewart; we depend on each other. The hours are long, the work is bloody hard and the odds, you might as well know right now, are often against us.'

'So what's new?' She hurried after him, almost running to keep up with his lengthy stride. The automatic doors opened and she stepped outside, gasping involuntarily as a wave of heat struck her forcibly. She felt strangely light-headed and already her shirt was sticking to her.

'*This* is what's new.' Sam Brady's dark eyes skimmed sardonically over her, seeing the faint sheen of exhaustion on her pale skin. 'This is hot. Believe me, it will get a lot hotter.'

A wave of dizziness swept over her. She moistened her dry lips with her tongue, wishing that she could sit down, if only for a few minutes, just long enough to get herself together. Everything was happening too fast.

'I'll cope,' she forced out. 'I'm tougher than I look. I can take care of myself.'

This time the dark eyes narrowed cynically. 'I doubt it, Dr Stewart, and the fact is I'm responsible for every member of the team and I don't have time to play nursemaid.'

She came to an abrupt halt and wished she hadn't as her head seemed to swim. 'So, what are you suggesting?

That I hang around the airport and take the first available flight out?'

The mere thought made her feel faint. Damn Sam Brady! The man didn't even know her, yet already he had her categorised and she wasn't even being given a chance to defend herself. In an unconscious gesture she ran a hand through her hair and his eyes narrowed.

'Don't think I'm not tempted, Dr Stewart. Unfortunately, it isn't quite that simple. I'm short of staff as it is. Those I do have are overworked. So, while nothing would give me greater pleasure than to see you head back to where you came from, right now it looks as if we're stuck with each other. At least until I can get a suitable replacement.'

He came to a halt beside a dust-covered Land Rover, opened the door and waited. He looked tough, the thought invaded her senses. The sort of man it would be good to have on your side in moments of trouble. It was a pity he didn't like her but, then, she didn't need looking after. She simply had to work with the man and, provided she did her job, he wouldn't have reason to complain.

Even so, for a few seconds she toyed with the idea of telling him to go to hell.

'I suggest we make a move. It'll be dark soon and we still have some distance to cover.' His eyes glinted. 'Unless, of course, you feel able to cope with a night out in the open, beneath the stars?'

'That won't be necessary, thank you.' Gritting her teeth, she climbed into the vehicle. 'Just take me to my hotel. All I need right now is a shower and some sleep. After that I'll be ready to start whenever you are.'

'I hate to disappoint you—' the blue eyes contained a definite hint of humour as he swung her luggage into the back before climbing into the driver's seat '—but there's been a slight change of plan. You won't be staying in town after all.'

'But. . .I don't understand.' Her jaded spirits took a further dive. 'The arrangements were all made.'

'I'm sorry if it's inconvenient.' He gave a lazy grin and her breath caught in her throat at the realisation that she actually found this man sexually attractive.

'You'll be able to relax once we get to Ramindi. We *are* going to the hotel, but only long enough for me to pick up some mail and meet a representative from the health commission. After that we'll be heading straight back to the hospital. With luck we should be in Ramindi by nightfall.'

'I see.' Her mouth felt dry but she was determined not to let him guess that she couldn't take anything he cared to dish out. She had met Sam Brady's type before. Macho man!

With an effort she managed to keep her voice even. 'In that case, perhaps we should get going.' She clamped her lips together, deliberately turning her head to stare out of the window as he began to manoeuvre through the traffic. She wondered, briefly, what he would say if she told him that she felt faint and guessed that it wouldn't be a good idea.

He steered the vehicle easily through the busy streets and she was glad just to concentrate her attention on her first real glimpse of Nairobi as he did so. She didn't quite know what she had expected but it certainly wasn't this clean, modern city where brilliantly coloured hibiscus vied with bougainvillea and the vivid blue of flowering jacaranda trees made splashes of colour against giant skyscrapers and modern hotels.

'It's beautiful,' she murmured involuntarily.

'What did you expect? Camp-fires and a few mud huts?' He laughed, a deep-throated, surprisingly pleasant sound. 'Seriously, Nairobi comes as a surprise to most people coming here for the first time.' He glanced briefly in her direction.

'Take my advice—make the most of it because

Ramindi is another world.' His mouth twisted. 'We do the best we can with facilities that are pretty basic by any standards, and if you've a craving for any kind of social life then I'm afraid you're in for a disappointment. It's all down to us. Not that you'll have much time for relaxing.'

Colour flared into her cheeks. 'Don't worry, Dr Brady. I'm here to work, even if you do seem to be having difficulty accepting the idea. It may surprise you to know that I didn't even pack my party dress.'

His mouth twisted in a wry grin. 'Are you always this touchy?'

Her gaze flew up to meet his and found his eyes regarding her with mocking amusement. She was suddenly conscious of a crazy and totally illogical vortex of emotions that surged over her like a huge tidal wave as she looked up into the inky blue eyes and saw his mouth curve in silent laughter.

'I'm tired,' she said flatly. 'It was a long flight.' Too long. She had had too much time to think, mostly about Jeremy. She tilted her head back against the seat, closing her eyes and deliberately shutting Sam Brady out, wearily oblivious to their steady progress through the traffic. Coming to Africa was supposed to be an escape, a fresh start. The last thing she needed was to exchange one set of problems for another.

Without even being aware of it, she sighed. At the sound he turned his head, his gaze resting briefly on her pale features, the shadows beneath her eyes, and his dark brows drew together as he brought the vehicle to a halt, cutting the engine.

With an effort she dragged her eyes open to look around her. 'Are we there?'

'This is the hotel. It shouldn't take too long to do what I have to do.'

'I'll be fine,' she murmured, suddenly wishing her head wouldn't spin so. She wanted to tell him to take all the time he needed if it meant she could sleep. 'I'll wait here.'

'You'll wait inside.' His voice brooked no argument and she gasped slightly as his hand cupped her elbow. Almost before she could gather her senses, he was propelling her towards the large plate-glass doors of the hotel. 'It's cooler inside. I'll get someone to bring you a large, iced fruit juice. Drink it all.'

Yes, sir. No, sir. Three bags full. The thought rattled around inside her head so that she giggled—until a wave of dizziness swept over her, causing her to sway briefly.

Involuntarily she reached out and was held and instantly drawn against the taut, muscular body.

'Are you all right?' His hands caught her arms when she would have pulled away. She was vaguely aware of him frowning. He was too close. She could smell the subtle undertones of the aftershave he was wearing. It was nice, musky. Jeremy had always preferred more spicy fragrances. . .

It was galling to discover that her hands were actually shaking as, breathing hard, she drew herself up and free of his grasp. What must he be thinking? This was hardly the impression she had hoped to create on her first day in her new job.

'I'm fine, absolutely fine, Dr Brady,' she declared roundly, before slumping gently to the ground in a dead faint.

She lay fighting the mists that seem to be fogging her brain. Her head ached and she felt sick. What had happened? One minute she was holding a perfectly normal conversation and the next. . .

'Oh, *no*!' she groaned as dawning memory returned, bringing with it the startling realisation that Sam Brady was bending over her and fumbling with the buttons of her shirt. With a cry of protest she made a feeble attempt to stop him.

'What are you doing?' She pushed him firmly away, struggling dizzily to sit up.

'I wouldn't do that. . .'

The warning came too late. Sam's mouth indented briefly as he watched the sudden tide of colour wash from her cheeks as, with a groan of dismay, she pressed a hand to her mouth and sank back against the pillows.

'I did try to warn you.'

Kate swallowed hard. 'What happened? Where am I?'

'You fainted.' His brow rose quizzically. 'I was trying to loosen your clothing. It's standard procedure: loosen the clothing. . .'

'I know what the procedure is.' She peered witheringly in his direction. 'I've never fainted before in my life,' she ground out. 'I'm not the fainting type.'

'There's always a first time.' He stood looking down at her and then, as she pressed a hand to her throbbing head, moved to draw the curtains, shutting out the light. His mouth was grim as he returned to study her pale features. 'When did you last sleep—or eat, for that matter?'

'I. . .I don't remember precisely.'

His brows drew into a grim frown and she wished the words unsaid as his mouth tightened ominously. 'I might have guessed. Well, I don't know what kind of discipline you're used to, Dr Stewart, though I can guess, but out here we play by a different set of rules and the sooner you know them the better. There are thousands of people out there, battling just to stay alive.

'Rule one is that, from now on, you eat and drink on a regular basis, whether you feel like it or not. Didn't anyone ever tell you about the dangers of dehydration?'

'Yes, of course, but. . .'

'You're no use to anyone if you can't stay on your

feet.' He wasn't even giving her a chance to answer. 'Here, you'd better take these.' He thrust two tablets into her hand, followed by a glass of iced water. His hand was at the back of her head, practically forcing the liquid down her throat. Sam Brady was a bully, she decided, but she felt too tired to argue.

'My headache is much better,' she lied feebly as the water slid, blissfully cool, down her parched throat.

'You're not a very good liar, Dr Stewart.'

Indignation darkened her cheeks but he ignored it, removing the glass briskly from her hand. 'I've spoken to the hotel manager and arranged for a tray of food and a Thermos of juice to be sent up. I suggest you eat, drink and get a good night's sleep.'

She stared at him through eyes which suddenly seemed ridiculously full of tears. 'But I thought. . . Your meeting. . .'

'It's taken care of. As it happens, the commissioner I'm meeting was delayed anyway. He's waiting downstairs. We'll discuss what needs to be discussed over a meal, then hopefully I'll be able to get some sleep too.'

Kate stared at him, noting for the first time the tiny lines of exhaustion around his eyes and his mouth, and she sensed that while he might be hard on those around him Sam Brady was no less hard on himself.

'Look, I'm sorry.' She licked her dry lips. 'I didn't intend for this to happen. I realise you don't want me here, Dr Brady, but I can assure you I have every intention of pulling my weight. . .'

His mouth, a taut line of weariness, relaxed suddenly. 'I'm glad to hear it. Out here we work as a team. We rely on everyone doing their job.'

She looked at him steadily. 'And all I'm asking is a chance to prove that I can do mine. Perhaps it will help if you think of me as a doctor and not as a woman.'

A nerve pulsed in his jaw and Kate felt a tremor run through her as he looked at her with brooding eyes.

'I'll try to do that,' he ground out. There was something suspiciously akin to humour in the blue eyes as he moved towards the door.

'And you'll get your chance. By my estimation, you'll last about a month—then you'll be begging to be sent home. Oh, and by the way, the name's Sam. Since we're going to be working together you might as well get used to it.' He turned and strode to the door before turning to look at her.

'Give it some thought, Dr Stewart, then I suggest you get a good night's sleep. I leave for Ramindi at first light, with or without you.' Then he was gone.

Kate's first impulse, as she stared at the retreating figure, was to tell herself that he could go to hell and good riddance. But then, she realised, that was probably just what he wanted.

Her chin rose stubbornly. Well, she had a surprise for him. Right now they might be stuck with each other but, just as long as she was here, she had every intention of making Dr Sam Brady eat his words.

He was standing beside the ancient Land Rover next morning when, having gulped down a couple of aspirins with the dregs of her coffee, she hitched her bag firmly onto her shoulder and hurried out of the hotel.

There was a slight chill to the dawn air which took her by surprise and she was glad that she had thought to bring a light jacket with her.

'Good morning.' Feeling surprisingly refreshed, despite the lingering remnants of a headache, she was able to inject a genuinely pleasant note into the ritual greeting and, for a few seconds, his gaze seemed to linger on the stone-coloured trousers she had elected to wear.

They might be hot and not particularly fashionable, but at least they were sensible and offered some protection to her legs against the sun and the voracious army of insects which she had already discovered were so prevalent.

She had chosen to wear the coral-coloured shirt for the same reason. Its short, turned-back sleeves left her arms exposed, but her neck and shoulders remained protected. Let him find fault with that, she thought, swinging her bag onto the seat with a hint of defiance before climbing in herself.

Her hair she had simply tugged back, securing it with a gauzy, coloured scarf, until she became aware, beneath that cool gaze, of the escaping tendrils. Rebelliously she pulled a white cotton hat firmly down on her head.

'Sleep well?' Sam slung her suitcase into the back, tossing in his own gear before getting in beside her.

'Like a log, thanks. The jet lag must finally have caught up. I went out like a light.'

'Either that or the sleeping tablets did what they were supposed to do.' A small grin played around his mouth as he glanced in her direction.

She shot him a look of disbelief, hanging on as they set off. 'You wouldn't!'

'You needed to sleep.'

She felt outraged. 'So the end justifies the means— is that what you're saying?'

'Sometimes.' There was a certain malicious satisfaction in his voice as he said it and she choked on a reply, too intent on keeping a distance between them as he steered deftly through the light early-morning traffic until finally they reached the outskirts of the town.

'It gets a little rough from here on.' He shot her a quick glance as, without warning, the ancient vehicle lurched over a rut in the road, sending her sprawling against him.

Her outflung hand encountered warm, solid male chest.

He gave a lazy grin. 'Better hang on. It's going to get a lot rougher yet.'

She pushed herself away, scrambling with undignified haste back to her own side of the seat. 'Is this the best transport you've got?'

'It's the only transport.'

She flung him a look as she clung to the rattling doorframe. She wouldn't have put it past Sam Brady to have devised this form of torture solely for her benefit. But when she stole a look in his direction he was concentrating on keeping the vehicle steady on the track, his tanned hands remarkably relaxed as they gripped the wheel.

'It might not look much, but it serves its purpose. Once you leave the towns most of the roads are little more than dust tracks.' He brushed the back of his arm against his forehead, wiping away a film of sweat. 'We're lucky. Most of the patients who come to Ramindi for treatment have to walk, sometimes for days, sometimes carrying children or elderly relatives.'

Kate frowned, flapping a persistent cloud of flies away from her face. 'I take it you hold clinics?'

'Of course, and then we use the bigger medical truck. But when you're trying to cover an area as large as we have to there's a limit to how often you can visit every outlying village or township.' His mouth tightened briefly. 'We do the best we can. I know damn well it's not enough. It'll never be enough.'

Kate turned, surreptitiously, to study his profile and was devastated to meet his blue eyes. 'If you really believe that, why go on?'

'Someone has to. I'm not saying it's all for nothing. Every day brings a new miracle. But then you know there's going to be the next day, and the day after that. There's always another patient—another thousand patients.'

She frowned, moved by the obvious depths of his concern. 'So, how do you cope?'

'We get on with it because there's nothing else to do.' His mouth twisted. 'Believe me, death out here is on a scale you never dreamed of.' He took his eyes off the track to glance briefly in her direction.

'If I've seemed over-harsh it's because you'll see suffering out here that you couldn't even begin to imagine, and you can't run away from it just because you feel squeamish or pick up the phone because you feel homesick.'

Kate drew a sharp breath. 'And you think that's what I'll do? How can you make a judgement like that? You don't even know me.'

'You aren't the first and you won't be the last doctor to come out here filled with a pioneering spirit, thinking you can perform a few miracles and make everything right.'

She turned to look at him. 'I don't expect to perform miracles. But surely I have at least the right to try. . . to do something?'

He smiled faintly at that. 'Like I said, I'll give you a month and you'll be crying yourself to sleep. You'll become a liability, Dr Stewart.'

'Maybe I'm tougher than I look.'

'For your sake I can only hope that's true.' He turned away to concentrate on keeping the vehicle steady on the track and her gaze returned to his profile.

His dark hair curled slightly against the collar of the shirt he was wearing. Behind his rugged face and slightly sensual mouth was a streak of stubbornness, she thought. Sam Brady could be quite ruthless—of that she had no doubt.

She brushed the back of her hand against her forehead. She felt hot and sticky. Already dust seemed to clog every pore and clung to her hair.

Her thoughts strayed briefly to England and in

particular to Foxleigh, the small village where she lived.
It was probably raining, or snowing, even. She pushed
the tantalising image away. She had promised herself
that she wasn't going to think about home. She had
wanted a fresh start—a new challenge—and, whether
she liked him or not, Sam Brady was part of that challenge. She wasn't about to prove him right by allowing
herself to be defeated by homesickness before she had
even unpacked.

She eased her blouse away from her skin, feeling the
thin trickle of sweat between her shoulder-blades as she
turned to look at him. 'I gather you're concentrating on
an immunisation programme at the moment? I suppose
measles is a major problem?'

'Measles, polio, malaria, tuberculosis.' He gave a
wry smile. 'You name it, we deal with it.'

Kate frowned. 'TB is on the increase at home too.
I'm not sure why.'

'It's simple enough. More people are living rough.
If they can't find work they don't have the money to
spend on a decent diet. If you're under-nourished you're
more susceptible. As a doctor, surely you must
know that?'

'Yes, of course.' Colour surged into her cheeks. 'It
just takes some getting used to, in this day and age,
that's all. TB was something my parents and grand-
parents knew all about. By the time I grew up the theory
was that it had been virtually wiped out, except that I
know we've been seeing more cases admitted to
hospital.'

'At least these days, with effective drugs and chemo-
therapy, the death rate from pulmonary tuberculosis is
practically nil.'

'Provided the bacilli don't turn out to be drug-
resistant.'

Blue eyes glinted as Sam shot a look in her direction.
'Well done, Dr Stewart.'

For some ridiculous reason the quietly spoken words sent a tiny frisson of pleasure running through her and, with it, a small spark of resentment.

She flashed him a look. 'I'm glad I passed the test. I take it that's what it was—a test of my professional capabilities?'

He gave a slight laugh. 'I hate to shatter your illusions, but no amount of theory can make up for practical experience.' He shifted his gaze back to the road ahead. 'Try to relax. We still have a way to go.'

Relax? How could she relax? There was nothing even remotely relaxing about Sam Brady. She looked away quickly as he glanced at her, as if aware of her silent appraisal, and her heart gave an odd little leap.

Sam Brady bothered her. For some reason he had the disconcerting ability to make her feel vulnerable. The sooner they reached Ramindi and she could throw herself into her work, she decided, the better.

Within the space of an hour the sun's heat had become intense. Conversation died away as Sam concentrated all his energies on keeping the vehicle on the dirt road, leaving Kate to stare out of the open window at a cloudless sky.

Flapping a hand desultorily at the seemingly endless swarm of flies, she gazed into the hazy distance across a scrubland of dark acacias and yellow grass, broken every now and again by small clumps of trees and flat-roofed huts.

Occasionally figures dressed in tasselled brown cloaks, their necks and ankles adorned with jewellery, were to be seen herding small flocks of goats or cattle.

Gradually a feeling of lethargy stole over her. She brushed a hand through her hair. Her eyes closed briefly against the stinging dust. What she needed more than anything right now was a long cold shower, a bed with cool sheets and a soft pillow.

'That's Ramindi ahead.'

At the sound of the voice her eyes flew open and she became aware of the fact that her head was resting against something solid.

She must have fallen asleep and the something solid was Sam's shoulder, the muscles tensing as he manoeuvred the Land Rover through a dry gully. With a dawning realisation she jerked upright, moving away, but not before she found herself looking directly into the blue eyes and felt herself blush. 'I'm sorry.' She moistened her dry lips with her tongue. 'I must have dozed off.'

He gave a lazy grin and she was horrified to feel her body quiver with awareness. 'You slept for an hour.' He nodded ahead. 'That's Ramindi. We should be there in about five minutes.'

She followed his gaze, not sure whether it was relief or trepidation she felt as he swung the vehicle in a trail of dust into the compound and came to a halt.

CHAPTER THREE

RAMINDI seemed to consist of several wooden bungalows, some higher up on the slopes, shaded by trees
beneath which sat small groups of women and children.
Several of the bungalows had small verandas and it was
from one of these that a figure emerged, shading her
eyes from the sun to watch their arrival and then, as
recognition dawned, hurrying down the steps to
meet them.

She was wearing a white, short-sleeved dress with a
neat navy belt cinching in the waist, her short, blonde
hair neatly bobbed.

'Hi,' she greeted Sam. 'How was the trip?'

'Productive.' Sam leaned into the Land Rover,
deposited Kate's luggage on the ground and then
reached in again for a large cool-box which he placed,
grinning, in the girl's arms. 'Goodies.'

'The vaccines! Oh, thank goodness.'

'There's more.' With a slight grin he dropped a
bundle of assorted envelopes on top of the box.

'*Mail!* Sam, you're my very favourite person in all
the world. But how. . .?' Frowning, she tapped the
insulated box.

'Courtesy of an obliging hotel manager who allowed
me the use of a refrigerator for overnight storage.'

'We were beginning to wonder what had happened
to you.' She chuckled, her tanned features emphasising
even, white teeth. 'We were taking bets that you'd
decided to take a little unofficial leave.'

Kate looked anxiously from one to the other. 'I'm
afraid I might have been responsible for the change in
plans,' she began apologetically.

The girl's smile was at once friendly and full of curiosity. 'Hey, don't worry about it.' She grinned. 'Getting Sam to take leave would be like some kind of miracle. Welcome to Ramindi, by the way. I'm Jill Forbes.' She held out her hand as Sam made the introductions.

'This is Dr Stewart. Jill is our senior sister. She practically runs the place. I doubt if we'd survive without her.'

'He says the nicest things.' Jill grinned. 'Hi again. I can't tell you how glad we are to have you here. I expect Sam's told you we need all the help we can get. I just hope he hasn't managed to put you off.'

Deliberately ignoring Sam's gaze, Kate gave a wry smile. 'I gather things are pretty hectic—and the name is Kate, by the way.'

'How was the flight?'

'Boring. I can't tell you how good it is to be here and, no, he hasn't managed to put me off—not so far, anyway. I've been looking forward to a new challenge. I can't wait to get started,' Kate smilingly assured her.

'Perhaps you should wait until you've seen precisely what you're letting yourself in for.' Sam's mouth twisted derisively. 'You might still have second thoughts.'

'I don't think so.' Her chin rose defensively but it seemed he wasn't even listening as he glanced, frowning, at his watch.

'I'm due in clinic. How's Ben?'

Jill Forbes frowned. 'I saw him about half an hour ago. I'm afraid he's still very poorly.'

'*Damn!*' He swore softly under his breath. 'Is he still vomiting?'

Jill nodded.

'And what about the test results?'

'They came through first thing this morning. Positive, I'm afraid. As you suspected.'

'*Hell!*' He raked a hand through his hair. 'I'd better

get over there. Who's taking the out-patients' clinic?'

'Dr Ahmed.'

'And what about the mums and babies?'

'Greg said to tell you not to worry. He's coping. Sister Wande is helping out.'

Kate's troubled gaze shifted from one to the other. 'Look, there's obviously a problem. I feel at least partly responsible.' She bit at her lower lip. 'There must be something I can do to help.'

Sam flung a look in her direction. 'Right now the most helpful thing you can do is get something to eat, take a shower and get some rest. Jill will show you to your quarters.'

'But I don't need a rest.' She felt the warm colour surge into her cheeks. 'I want to help. It is what I'm here for, after all.'

His blue gaze narrowed. 'You'll help best by following orders, Doctor. You'll be no good to the patients or yourself if you can't stay on your feet. Tomorrow morning will be soon enough to report for duty.'

He was gone, striding away before she could speak, and she stood, rooted to the spot, feeling a tide of anger and frustration wash over her.

Jill turned uncertainly to Kate. 'Are you all right?'

'What? Oh, yes, at least I think so.' In a weary gesture, Kate ran a hand through her hair as she tried to gather her thoughts into some semblance of order.

She had left England full of enthusiasm for her new job, telling herself that she was actually going to be doing something worthwhile. What she hadn't counted on was meeting an immovable force like Sam Brady, who seemed to have made up his mind in advance that, as a doctor, her talents were next to useless and he wasn't prepared to give her a chance to prove otherwise.

Jill gave a wry smile as she led the way towards one of the smaller bungalows. 'Am I imagining things, or do I detect a certain tension?'

Kate gave a slight laugh, taking an instant liking to the girl who seemed about her own age. 'You could say we got off on slightly the wrong foot,' she managed lightly. 'I'm not sure quite what Dr Brady was expecting. I just get the distinct impression that I'm not it.'

Jill smiled as she led the way up the steps. 'I know Sam can sometimes seem a little abrupt, but don't take it to heart. He's a good doctor and once you get to know him he's actually very nice.'

'Yes, well, I'll take your word for it.'

Jill gave another wry smile. 'Things have been pretty hectic here for the past few months. Sam's had a tough time of it since George went back to England.'

'Yes, I heard there was a problem. I didn't know what. . .'

Jill waved a greeting to a passing nurse. 'George had arthritis. It didn't affect him too badly in the beginning and George, being George, insisted on soldiering on, but it started to affect his hips. I think he thought if he ignored it long enough it would go away, especially when Sam came out to act as deputy medical officer. Unfortunately things had begun to get somewhat neglected.' She pulled a face. 'It was Sam who realised that things were getting too much for George.'

'I can see it might create a few problems. What happened?'

Jill shrugged. 'George finally admitted defeat. He went back to the UK three months ago for hip replacements and Sam took over here. It was the logical solution. I mean, he'd been covering for George and virtually keeping the place running, anyway.' She led the way along a small veranda. 'Look, let's get you settled. You must be dying for a shower and a cup of tea.' She pushed open a door. 'This is yours. It's fairly basic, I'm afraid. The one consolation is that you won't be spending too much time in here.'

Kate dropped her bag onto the bed and looked around, taking in the brightly coloured curtains and matching cotton bedspread, a chest of drawers, small table and chair.

'It's fine,' she pronounced. 'It's cool and it has everything I'm likely to need.' Once she had unpacked her clothes and the few books and personal items she had brought with her, she crossed to the window, looking out across the compound.

'How many wards are there?'

'Five. I'll show you around later, if you like. Introduce you to some of the people you'll be working with. But there's really no rush. No one seriously expects you to put in an appearance, officially at any rate, for the first twenty-four hours.' She grinned. 'I seem to remember I wasn't capable even if I'd wanted to. It took me a week to remember what day it was. Why don't you try to get some sleep?'

'I doubt if I could even if I tried,' Kate smiled. 'I feel as if my head is still back in England. Anyway, I'd like to get started.'

The other girl grinned appreciatively. 'Well, I won't pretend another pair of hands won't be appreciated.' She paused at the door, her expression sobering slightly.

'I meant it, you know. Sam really is OK. You caught him at a bad time. We've had an influx of cholera cases from up-country, refugees mostly. On top of that he's been worried sick about young Ben.' She gave a lopsided smile. 'I suppose, basically, what I'm trying to say is that we're lucky to have him.'

Kate determinedly swept aside an image of the ruggedly attractive features and compelling blue eyes. Sam Brady might be the best doctor in the world—she could go along with that. It was the idea of him as Mr Nice Guy she was having trouble with.

She frowned. 'Who exactly is Ben? I heard you mention him earlier.'

Jill pulled a face. 'He's a three-year-old. Well, at least we *think* he's three. He was admitted a couple of days ago with his mother. As far as we can make out, she had been walking for days and was in a state of extreme malnutrition herself. If she hadn't been picked up by one of the aid trucks, I doubt whether she would have made it to the hospital.' She flapped her hand at a fly.

'What was the problem?'

'It was pretty obvious that the child was seriously ill. Sam examined him and confirmed the diagnosis—cerebral malaria.'

'Oh, no! How is he?'

The other girl gave a shrug. 'Very poorly. Sam started him on chloroquine straight away. The problem, as you'll know, is that the malarial parasite can develop a resistance to the drug, which isn't making things any easier.'

'And is that what's happening in Ben's case?'

'It looks pretty much like it. In which case, Sam's going to have to have a rethink.' Jill sighed. 'Which is why he's a shade more edgy than usual.'

Kate sat on the bed. 'What do you reckon are his chances?'

'He hasn't got a lot going for him, but he's in the best possible hands. Sam isn't a quitter. He won't give up easily.'

No, Kate thought, she could well believe it. It also explained a part, if not all, of the reason for his apparent hostility since their meeting.

Jill glanced at her watch. 'Lor, I'm due on the ward in fifteen minutes. Look, why not come over with me now—or would you prefer to settle in, take a shower then see how you feel? Don't be afraid to crash out if that's what you'd rather do. We've all done the jet lag bit so no one will think any the worse of you.'

Except Sam Brady, maybe. Kate pushed the thought

away, smiling. 'Thanks, I'll come with you, if you don't mind, and I'm grateful.'

'Hey, it's good to have you here.'

Hastily rummaging in her bag, Kate found a white coat, shrugging herself into it as they ran lightly down the steps together into the brilliant sunshine.

'You said there are five wards?'

'That's right. Male, Female, Mums and Babies, Post-op and Obstetrics,' Jill smilingly explained as they skirted a noisy group, mainly women with small children, heading towards a cluster of bungalows. 'Or, at least, that's the theory. We also hold two clinics a day. That's why most of these people are here.' She called out a greeting and the women responded, waving and smiling.

'You start work pretty early.'

'It's a case of getting through as much of the work as possible in the coolest part of the day. It's hot now but it could get pretty unbearable later.'

Kate could believe it. A thin trickle of sweat was already making its presence felt between her shoulder-blades.

'We're through here.' Jill led the way through the door leading to the ward, almost colliding with an escaping toddler. The young nurse in hot pursuit laughingly scooped him up. 'Ingabire, there's someone I'd like you to meet. This is our latest recruit, Dr Kate Stewart from England. Dr Stewart, this is Ingabire, one of our senior staff nurses.'

The girl smiled shyly, showing even white teeth. 'Dr Stewart.'

Kate smiled at the infant who stuck his fingers in his mouth as he regarded them solemnly. 'It looks as if you have your hands pretty full.'

Jill grinned. 'Ingabire has been at Ramindi for almost a year now. In fact, we arrived at pretty much the same time. The children all think the world of her and, frankly, we couldn't manage without her.' To the girl she said, 'I'm just going to show Dr Stewart around and introduce her to some of the patients. By the way, how's Thomas?' She glanced at her watch. 'He must be out of Theatre by now?'

'Half an hour ago,' the girl smiled. 'He's still in Recovery. Dr Brady looked in on him a while ago. He's doing fine.'

'Good. Let me know as soon as he comes back onto the ward and I'll take a look at him.'

The girl hurried away, the infant still balanced on her hip, playfully trying to catch at the colourful scarf she had used to cover her hair.

Jill led the way to a small area at the end of the ward. 'This is the office,' she grinned as she indicated a small desk which had certainly seen better days. 'As you'll see, I use the word advisedly. Not exactly the ultimate in modern design, I'm afraid.' She slid open one of the drawers in an equally ancient filing cabinet. 'And patients' records are kept in here.'

'How many patients do you have on each ward?'

'Thirty-five. It's all we have room for and it's never enough. Occupancy is always one hundred per cent. There's no such thing as an empty bed. We discharge a patient and admit another straight away.'

'So what happens in an emergency?'

Jill smiled wryly, flipping through a bundle of case note files and dropping them onto the desk. 'It would be difficult to say what counts as an emergency. Most of the cases we get are urgent in one way or another. Young Thomas is a case in point.'

'What's wrong with him?'

'Onchocerciasis.'

Kate frowned. 'That's. . .caused by worms?'

'That's right. The infection is spread by the bite of a small fly. It breeds in streams and is caused by the filarial worm, *onchocerca volvulus*. The parasite lives in small lumps or nodules, usually around the head, chest wall, knees or elbows.'

Kate nodded. 'I haven't seen too many cases but I seem to recall that the affected areas of skin are lighter in colour.'

'That's right.' Jill handed her the case notes and Kate scanned the card, frowning.

'I take it that's why he was in surgery? To have the nodules removed? What about follow-up treatment?'

'He'll be given a course of diethylcarbamazine.'

Kate handed back the card. 'So how do you decide which case should take priority?'

'We don't.' Jill smiled. 'Don't worry about it. It's first come first served. Well, almost. I know it probably all seems fairly laid back, but the system seems to work. You'll soon get used to it.'

Kate laughed. 'I hope you're right.'

'Ah, and here's someone you definitely should meet. Let's grab him while he's here. The man's a positive whirlwind; heaven knows when you may get the chance again.'

With Kate at her heels she sped in pursuit of a tall, sandy-haired figure in a white coat. 'Greg, I thought you'd like to meet our new arrival. Dr Stewart, Greg Cooper. . .our second in command, so to speak. . .'

'And general dogsbody.' Brown eyes twinkled as he finished writing his notes and turned towards Kate. He was about thirty-five years old, tanned and good-looking. 'Always a pleasure to welcome a new face.' One eyebrow rose as he extended his hand in welcome. 'Dr Stewart.' His voice bore a strong trace of a Canadian accent. 'Especially when it's a pretty face.'

Kate laughed as her hand was clasped in a strong, warm grip. 'Dr Cooper.'

'Greg, *please*. Let's start the way we mean to go on.'

'In that case, the name is Kate.'

'I just know we're going to get along.' He still

retained his grasp of her hand. 'Perhaps we can get together some time and discuss cases?'

'Ignore him.' Jill's eyes twinkled. 'He's incorrigible.'

'I have to plead guilty.' Greg Cooper grinned. 'Seriously, though, you'll probably get sick of hearing it, but we need all the help we can get.'

'I'm just showing Kate around, introducing her to the patients and some of the team. I don't suppose you've seen Sam anywhere?'

'Not since first thing.' He smiled at Kate. 'I hate to rush away but. . .' he gave an exaggerated sigh '. . .right now I'm supposed to be lancing a boil. I'll probably catch up with you later.'

'I'll look forward to it.'

He sped away and Jill smiled. 'He's harmless, I promise. Just take everything he says with a pinch of salt.' She led the way along the ward, pausing at the foot of one of the metal-framed beds to unclip the chart. She handed it, with a small buff folder, to Kate. 'This is Hirigo. He came to us three days ago. He's still very poorly.'

Kate glanced at the notes and moved to the side of the bed, glancing down at the child who was sleeping restlessly, one thin arm flung across his face. Automatically she checked his pulse and said softly, 'How old is he? Eighteen months? Two years?'

'He's four.'

Kate stared at her, studying the notes again, biting at her lower lip. 'I see he has PEM. Protein-energy malnutrition.' She released a pent-up breath. 'Well, that certainly explains his poor size.' She flipped the page again. 'He has kwashiorkor. That's a severe form of PEM.'

Jill nodded. 'The main cause is obviously poor diet but we usually find there are several causes. Poverty, cultural attitudes, an unwillingness, for instance, to give milk or fish and eggs because the parents think, wrongly, that they cause worms.'

'You're not serious?'

'I'm afraid so. In this case the reason is much more simple. It's down to a lack of breast milk when he was a baby.'

'You mean the mother couldn't feed him? But surely there are alternatives to breast milk?'

Jill shook her head. 'In Hirigo's case it was simply that his mother became pregnant again, so he was displaced by the new infant. It often happens and usually we find that the older child never makes up lost ground.'

Kate found herself having to battle hard against an unreasoning sense of frustration. It was no good letting it get to her. These were precisely the kind of things she was going to have to get used to if she was going to be able to work out here—she knew that.

None of her feelings was evident, however, as she leaned forward to gently press the child's swollen feet and legs. 'The oedema is pretty classic.' She studied the child's bright red tongue—proof of a lack of riboflavin—and the small skin ulcers and cracks in the skin before she straightened up.

'Poor little mite. He must be pretty miserable. I take it he's on a high-energy diet? The priority in the early stages is obviously in correcting the dehydration and medical imbalance.'

Jill nodded. 'We're giving him dilute feeds—half-strength milk formula to prevent diarrhoea and vomiting. By tomorrow, if all goes well, he'll be on full-strength milk mixed with sugar, oil and water. For the first couple of days we had to feed him by intragastric tube but he's improved sufficiently to be able to use a cup now—with help.'

Kate nodded, grateful already for the girl's obvious ready knowledge. 'The main problem, once he does start to pick up, will be to make sure the mother understands how to keep to a sensible diet once he is ready to go home.'

Jill gave a wry smile. 'That won't be easy.' She returned the clipboard to the end of the bed as they prepared to move on. 'She's pregnant again. This will be her fifth. Still, we do our best.'

They made a steady progress along the ward, pausing at each bed in turn until they came to the last.

'And this is little Ben.' Jill waited as a young nurse finished checking a drip before writing up the notes. Even now, though the sun was beginning to go down, the air was still heavy and a fan whirred steadily beside the bed.

'How is he?' Jill said softly.

The girl acknowledged their presence with a smile, then shook her head. 'About the same.'

Jill nodded. 'Nurse Kangwana, this is Dr Stewart, who's come from England to join us.'

'Welcome to Ramindi, Dr Stewart.' The girl smiled shyly before hurrying away with a bundle of soiled linen.

'You say he has cerebral malaria.' Kate gazed down at the child in the cot. His tiny, stick-like limbs were filmed with sweat yet he was shivering, turning his head restlessly from side to side. 'Do you mind if I take a look?'

'Go ahead.'

Kate watched the laboured rise and fall of the child's chest as her eyes made a quick but thorough assessment. She reached for his tiny wrist and felt the thready pulse. 'How long has he been like this?'

'This is the third day.'

Kate took the notes Jill proffered, glancing through them before handing them back. Gently she raised the infant's eyelids then studied his hands. 'Poor little chap.'

'So, what's your verdict, Doctor?'

Kate experienced a sense of shock as she realised that her early warning system, that tiny, nervous tingle that ran down her spine, had let her down as she glanced up slowly to see Sam Brady standing there.

She straightened up, feeling her heart give an illogical thud as she faced him. 'I haven't seen too many cases of cerebral malaria.'

'I'd be surprised if you had,' he said evenly. 'Unfortunately, out here it's all too common.' His blue eyes narrowed briefly, taking in her white coat, before he turned his attention back to the child who whimpered restlessly. 'Perhaps you'd care to complete your examination and offer a conclusion?'

He stood aside and, biting at her lower lip, she moved closer. Somehow, in the process, his hand brushed against her arm, sending a tiny sensation of shock running through her so that she was caught completely off guard by the way her pulse raced, totally illogically, at the brief contact.

It was impossible, in the confined space, to distance herself physically so she did the next best thing, by doing so mentally in a cloak of professionalism.

She was briefly aware of Jill making her excuses and slipping away as, taking her stethoscope from her pocket, she made a gentle but thorough examination. After several moments she straightened up, frowning, and met Sam's gaze.

'I'd say he has all the textbook symptoms. He's clearly anaemic and both the spleen and the liver are enlarged.'

He nodded, saying nothing.

'I. . .I'd guess that with a sustained high fever he's probably also suffered convulsions.'

Again he said nothing and she stifled a tiny feeling of resentment at being made to feel that she was, in some way, on trial. 'He probably has a history of bronchitis and diarrhoea.'

'Would you care to hazard a guess as to prognosis?'

Unconsciously she brushed a strand of hair from her eyes as she straightened and looked at him. 'I'd have to say it doesn't look too good.'

His eyes narrowed with sudden frustration. 'I'd be less polite and say it's bloody awful. Even if he makes it, the chances are he'll end up with permanent brain damage, probably mental deficiency and possibly paralysis of at least one limb.' He spread his hands in a gesture of impotence. 'This sort of thing shouldn't still be happening, but it is. I see it every day and there's not a damn thing I can do about it.'

'I'm sure you've done everything you could.'

'But it's not enough, is it?' His mouth twisted. 'In this day and age, knowing what we do and with all the drugs at our disposal, malaria should be a thing of the past—wiped out. Yet here it still exists on an unimaginable scale.' He looked around, his mouth tightening. 'Sometimes I feel I'm fighting a battle I can't ever win. Every piece of equipment we have is either obsolete by western standards or falling apart, and the irony is that we're damned glad to have it.'

Kate thought of the relatively modern, well-equipped hospital where she had done her own training. 'I'm almost ashamed at how much we take for granted. I hadn't realised. . .' She swallowed hard. 'I agree—it is unfair. But if you really do believe that what you're doing is such a waste of time, why stay? Why not just pack up and get out—go home?'

Blue eyes glinted. 'Probably because, occasionally—on a better than average day—I might just get the crazy idea that I'm still actually achieving something. And maybe because I don't know anyone else who'd be fool enough to take it on if I leave.' He gave a lazy grin and her breath caught in her throat. 'Maybe one of these days I'll put it to the test.'

So why didn't she believe it? Kate thought, struggling

to bring her thoughts under control as she looked at him. 'None of which actually answers the problem of what to do in this particular case.' She reached for the buff folder. 'I see from his notes that you've been using chloroquine. It's the standard procedure.'

Sam's mouth quirked. 'Except that it doesn't always work. In Ben's case it looks as if the parasites are resistant.'

Kate frowned. 'So, what happens now? Surely you're not suggesting that we just give up?'

'No, we don't give up,' came the quiet rejoinder. 'We try something else. I'm going to start him on a combination of pyrimethamine and sulphadoxine. I picked up some fresh supplies of drugs with the delivery of vaccines.'

She gave a sigh of relief. Suddenly it was as if the jet lag she had been fighting so hard to keep at bay had caught up on her with a vengeance. Exhaustion descended like a wave. She brushed a hand weakly against her forehead. Her face felt dewed with sweat and she had to swallow hard several times before the dryness in her mouth passed.

'I'm glad,' she managed evenly, going ahead of him as they moved away from the bed.

He held the curtain aside. 'Giving up isn't part of our remit, Dr Stewart, but the new treatment doesn't offer any guarantees.'

'Maybe not, but it has to be better than no chance at all.' She was vaguely aware of Sam's hand beneath her arm, leading her out of the ward.

They emerged into the rapidly fading light and she was glad of the faint breeze that hit her as she broke away from him to stand, gripping the veranda rail, breathing hard.

His gaze levelled with hers. 'Don't make the mistake of getting emotionally involved with your patients, Dr Stewart. If you do you'll only end up getting hurt.'

She felt the warm colour flare into her cheeks as she turned to look at him. 'Are you always so cynical?'

'I'm being realistic.' His voice hardened. 'Ben is just one case.'

'But he's still a baby.' She tried to move away but his hand caught her arm and he swung her to face him. She was conscious of a whole vortex of emotions that surged over her, leaving her feeling ridiculously breathless as she looked into his eyes.

'There are millions of babies. Hundreds die every day,' he said tautly, his hands on her arms now as he forced her to look at him. 'I don't like what's happening, but I'm a realist. I have to see the way things are. You may not like it but that's the way it is.' He stared down at her, his face taut. 'The drugs Ben will get won't be available to those other babies because they cost too much. When they run out, that's it.'

'Can't you order more?'

'Don't you think I would if it were that simple? Unfortunately it isn't. There's no blank cheque. We're kept afloat by a small grant and charitable donations, and we're not alone. There are too many others, just like us, all wanting a share of the cake.'

The intensity in his voice shook her and she frowned uncertainly. 'So you're saying it's all down to money?'

'Isn't everything, in the end? Maybe, someday, things will change. Until then we survive. We do the best we can.' He looked at her for a second. 'Take my word, you'll get used to it.'

She drew a breath and looked into the taut features, fighting a sudden and almost overwhelming sense of desolation. Her chin rose.

'I hope not,' she retorted, feeling the colour flare into her cheeks. 'God forbid I should ever take any of this for granted. You may have ice in your veins. I can't just ignore what's happening out here. I hope I never feel that way.'

His mouth twisted. 'You'll learn. You'll have to. If we worked twenty-four hours a day, every day, that queue of patients would still be there.' His eyes narrowed to glittering blue slits. 'As for having ice in my veins, Dr Stewart, well, perhaps we should put that to the test. I'd hate you to be under any illusions.'

Sam's hand closed on hers and instinctively she tried to pull away. For an instant she contemplated flight but knew that it wasn't even an option as the pressure of his hand became a light but determined statement of possession, drawing her inexorably closer. Warm colour flared in her cheeks as her body made sharp contact with his.

Shock briefly widened her eyes as, almost negligently, his finger traced the curve of her cheek. The sensual mouth was just a breath away, so close that her nostrils were invaded by the clean, musky smell of him.

Then she began to struggle as the sheer physical awareness of his body tore through her as he lowered his head and his mouth took possession of hers with an aggressive thoroughness that took her breath away, forcing her lips apart as his tongue savagely invaded the softness of her mouth.

She gasped at the contempt with which he took advantage of her own physical weakness. Then, to her everlasting shame, a totally new sensation coursed through her—so exquisite, so unlike anything she had ever experienced before, that she gasped again as her body betrayed her with its instant response .

She stood, mesmerised, stunned by the power of the sensations that coursed through her. His eyes really were incredibly blue. She stared at the thick lashes then, suddenly, she was struggling furiously to break free. What on earth was she thinking of? How could she love Jeremy yet feel so sexually excited by another man?

'How dare you?' She pushed him firmly away.

Blue eyes glinted as he released her, breathing hard. 'I

hate to disappoint you, Dr Stewart, but in every respect I am a perfectly healthy, full-blooded male. If you know what's good for you, I suggest in future that you remember that and don't,' he warned softly, 'offer challenges you can't back up. And now I suggest you get some sleep. It's been a long day. Tomorrow, you'll find out what Ramindi is really all about—if you think you're up to it.'

Without waiting to see the effect his words had, he turned on his heel and walked away, leaving her to stare after him.

'Well, really!' She swept a hand through her hair, guessing at how she must look. She felt as if she had been savaged. Her mouth felt swollen and her hair was still dishevelled where his hands had raked through it.

She had heard a lot about the dangerous wildlife in Africa. It was a pity no one had thought to warn her about Sam Brady!

CHAPTER FOUR

ALTHOUGH she hadn't expected to, Kate slept soundly for the first time in months. She woke next morning feeling surprisingly refreshed, having had none of the panic attacks she usually had when memories of Jeremy rushed in to leave her lying awake, feeling restless and exhausted and wondering how she was going to get through another day.

She had slept a dreamless sleep, aware—as her eyelids fluttered open and she lay, battling with a sense of disorientation—that something very nice had happened the night before. A dream, tantalising in its haziness.

She lay still for several seconds, listening to the incredible sounds of the animal and insect life as the African day got under way and trying to remember and to rebuild the fragmented images, and then, without warning, it all began to fall back into place.

Her heart gave an uncomfortable thud and she sat up quickly as memory suddenly returned, bringing the hot colour flaring into her cheeks. It hadn't been a dream. On the contrary, it was all too real, she remembered now. Sam Brady had kissed her! And he hadn't even bothered to be subtle about it.

She pushed back the sheet, hauling her mind swiftly back to safer ground. Sam Brady was a predator, she thought as, grabbing a towel, she headed for the shower to stand, gasping, beneath the needle-sharp jets of cold water. More than that, he was a predator of the worst kind; the sort who probably swallowed females for breakfast—any female—before moving on to the next.

Well, he wasn't going to get the chance with her, she decided as she towelled herself vigorously, taken

53

unawares as a fleeting but none the less disturbing
image of Sam Brady's attractive features flashed completely unbidden into her mind and she wondered briefly
what it would be like to be married to such a man.

She shook herself. What on earth was she doing,
daydreaming about a man she hardly knew? She
emerged from the shower on the surprisingly uncomfortable thought that he might be married anyway.

Having brushed her hair and slipped into a denim-
coloured skirt and short-sleeved white shirt, she went
out onto the veranda and stood looking at the scene
spread before her. The past few days had all been like
something of a dream but now, suddenly, the reality hit
her and she caught her breath at the sheer enormity
of it all.

As yet the air was still cool; there was even a slight
chill to it which took her by surprise as, having swallowed a cup of coffee, she made her way towards the
hospital.

The day's routine was obviously already well under
way as, breathlessly, Kate ran up the steps into the
small clinic.

'Sorry I'm late.'

'You're not.' Jill greeted her arrival with a smile as
she scrubbed her hands before checking the layout of
the instrument trolley. 'No one seriously expected you
to put in an appearance before midday. You should
have had a lie-in.'

'It's a nice thought but habit dies hard.' Kate grinned.
'I strongly suspect that as a medical student there were
times when I almost did a ward round in my sleep.'
She peered at the list Jill handed to her. 'So, what have
we got, then? From the look of things out there the
world and his wife are already beating a path to
the door.'

'You should see us on a bad day,' Jill chuckled.

'Don't worry about it. Out-patients is always one of our busiest clinics.'

And there's nothing like being dropped in at the deep end, is there, Sam? Kate thought, shrugging herself into her white coat and taking a deep breath. 'Right, let's make a start, then, shall we?' She gave a wry smile. 'Just stay close. This is not your average type casualty department. I'm way out of my depth here.'

Studying the small tray of very basic drugs and dressings which were available to her, she stifled a tiny feeling of depression as she seated herself at the well-scrubbed table and awaited the arrival of her first patient.

Several times that morning, as she worked her way steadily through a seemingly never-ending procession of patients, she felt a sense of gratitude to Jill and to Nziku Mitop, the young Tanzanian staff nurse who not only gently ushered patients in and out but also acted as interpreter.

Kate straightened up, easing her neck and shoulders briefly as she completed her examination of the man sitting hunched forward on the examination couch.

'All right, he can lie back now.' She smiled at the girl who helped him to rest against the pillows. The man was aged about fifty and, despite the fact that he was shivering, his skin was clammy and his breathing was shallow. 'What's his temperature?'

Frowning, Jill peered at the thermometer before shaking it down. 'A hundred and two.'

'Hmm.' Kate looked at Nziku. 'Ask him if he has any pain when he breathes in.' She waited for the girl to interpret and saw the man nod, pressing one hand lethargically to his chest. She glanced at the card. 'I see he's been coughing up blood. Do we know for how long?'

'It's all a bit vague, I'm afraid.'

Very gently, Kate palpated the man's abdomen and saw him wince. 'He's obviously getting some pain. He's very severely underweight too.' Reaching for her stethoscope, she listened intently to his chest, the whistling and bubbling sounds of congestion confirming her suspicions. 'I'd say he has pneumonia.'

'Do you want to get him admitted?'

'Yes, I think so. For a few days, anyway. We need to get the fever down and it will give us a chance to get some antibiotics into him.' She wrote up the notes. 'Better make sure his fluid intake is increased as well.'

'Will do.'

Kate smiled, waiting patiently as Nziku explained to the patient. He nodded as he was helped gently from the couch to be shown out and directed towards the main hospital block.

Scrubbing her hands in a small, cracked wash basin, Kate straightened her shoulders wearily for a moment. 'Don't you ever get the feeling that you're fighting a losing battle? Most of these people seem to have so little going for them. Poor diet, poor living conditions. . .'

'You just have to keep telling yourself that someday, hopefully, things will change.' Jill gave a slight smile.

'I should think even a born optimist might have trouble with that.' Kate gave a wry smile, pressing her damp hands to her warm face. 'Let's have the next one, shall we?'

She turned to smile reassuringly as the next patient was guided gently to the examination couch. There was no attempt at an answering smile. Mesianto Mengoru, who might have been anything between forty and sixty years old, was small and painfully underweight. She sat listlessly, eyes half-closed, one hand lifted occasionally to brush wearily over her face as Nziku spoke softly to her.

Kate glanced briefly at the card before saying gently, 'Can you tell me what is wrong?'

The woman pressed a clenched fist to her chest, making small beating movements. Kate glanced questioningly at Nziku.

'She says her heart beats too fast. She can no longer walk far to collect water. She has to rely on her daughter-in-law to fetch it for her.'

'I'd better have a listen to her chest.' Kate reached for her stethoscope, watching the woman carefully as she listened to the sluggish sounds of an enlarged heart. She frowned, straightening up. 'Does she have any pain anywhere?'

Nziku spoke to the woman who gestured lethargically towards her legs, rubbing her hands over the paper-thin skin.

'She says they stab and bite.'

Kate frowned until realisation dawned. 'Pins and needles?'

'I think so.'

Mesianto Mengoru spoke again, pinching at her leg.

'She says there is no feeling.'

'I'd better take a look.' Kate knelt to make her examination, running her hands gently over the emaciated limbs. 'There's definitely some oedema here. Here, too.' Straightening up, she examined the woman's face. 'Do we have any previous history? It would help if we knew when the symptoms started, although it could have been so gradual she might not have noticed.'

Jill hunted through the notes before shaking her head. 'There's nothing here.'

'What about relatives?'

'I think her daughter brought her to the hospital. Would you like Nziku to speak to her?'

Kate brushed her hand gently against the woman's skin. It felt cold and clammy. 'It might help if we explain the treatment. I think what we have here is a classic case of vitamin deficiency. It's important that she understands the importance of taking the medication.'

Sitting at the table, she wrote up the notes, glancing briefly at the tray of drugs. 'It would help if we knew how advanced the condition is. I'm pretty sure her heart is enlarged. Chances are she's going into heart failure.'

'Can you do anything?'

'I think so. In fact, the response to treatment is usually pretty dramatic and positive. Will you tell her that?'

Nziku held the woman's hand as she translated her words before straightening up to look at Kate. 'She says she has only her daughter-in-law to help her and the girl is lazy.'

Kate nodded sympathetically. 'Well, I'm afraid, for the time being at least, she's going to have to accept some help. She needs complete rest. I mean *complete* rest,' she emphasised. 'I'll write her up for thiamine, fifty milligrams, intramuscularly.' She looked at Jill.

'We'll admit her for three days and start that straight away. After that we'll follow up with tablets. Ten milligrams, three times a day. I'll need to see her again in about a month. Hopefully, by then there should be some significant improvement.'

For the rest of the morning they worked solidly until, by midday, the air was stifling. A small fan whirred ineffectively, disturbing warm air rather than bringing any real physical relief.

Kate raked a hand through the damp curls of her hair. Even tied back as it now was, the weight of it seemed to tug at her scalp, making her head ache, and she flexed her shoulders, attempting to ease the tension.

'Right, what's next?'

'Lunch.'

'But there's still a queue half a mile long.'

Jill completed her check of the supplies cupboard before closing her notebook with a satisfying thud. 'And it'll still be there when you come back.' She gave a rueful smile. 'It will always be there. You have to learn to switch off; to pace yourself. Come on.' She held open the door. 'Let's go and see what culinary wonders they've dreamed up for us today, and there's someone else you still have to meet.'

Wandering into the blissfully cool shade of the staff dining-room, Jill headed straight to where Greg was pouring coffee.

'Ah, you angel. Keep pouring. Black and three sugars.'

He looked up, grinning. 'I was just wondering whether to send out a search party. Here, you look as if you need it.' He handed Kate a cup. 'So, how was the first morning?'

'I'll tell you when I've recovered from the shock.' Easing off her shoes, she collapsed into a chair. 'Oh, that's bliss.'

'Bad as that?' Grinning, Greg spooned sugar into his own cup.

'It was an experience.' Sniffing appreciatively, she struggled to her feet again to investigate the appetising display of food which had been set out beneath mesh covers. 'Mmm, I hadn't realised how hungry I was until now.' She glanced up as another figure entered the dining-room.

'Ah, and here's the man himself. Sanje, come and meet our latest recruit. This is Dr Stewart—Kate Stewart.' Smiling, Jill made the introductions. 'Kate, meet Sanje Daliwhal—speciality orthopaedics, but has been known to turn his hand to most things.'

'Dr Stewart.' Brown eyes twinkled as Sanje extended his hand in greeting. Of Indian origin, tall and aged, Kate guessed, about forty, his thin, almost gaunt features were, at this moment, wreathed in a smile. 'Welcome to Ramindi. What are you making of us, I wonder?'

Kate smiled as her hand was clasped in a firm, warm grip. 'Dr Daliwhal.'

'Oh, no, please. Everyone calls me Sanje.'

'In that case the name is Kate.'

'I am so sorry not to be here when you arrived.'

She laughed. 'To tell you the truth I probably wouldn't have noticed. I was feeling a little dazed, to put it mildly. How long have you been here at Ramindi?'

'About six months.' He smiled, showing even, white teeth. 'Sometimes it seems much more.'

'Sanje did his medical training in Delhi,' Jill explained, helping herself to salad. 'I tell you because the man is too modest to tell you himself.'

'Because she is a bossy lady,' he grinned.

She shot him a look of mocking reproach. 'He was in general practice in England for two years before joining the team out here.'

'Really? Did you enjoy it?'

He laughed. 'It was a challenge and a valuable experience.'

Kate smiled. 'I'm sure it was. My father is a GP. I've helped him out occasionally. In fact, I did a month as locum before coming out here so I know how hectic it can be. Coffee?'

She held up the pot and was handing him a cup when the door opened and Sam walked in, a harassed expression marring his attractive features.

'I seem to spend more time on administration these days than doing the job I'm paid for.' There was a taut edge to his voice as he glanced up. 'If you're doing the honours I like mine black, no sugar.'

A small pulse began to hammer at the base of her throat as she poured the coffee, willing her hand not to shake as she handed him the cup.

As he took it their fingers met, invoking so vivid a memory of the few seconds she had spent in his arms that she jerked away, spilling coffee into the saucer.

Faded jeans hugged his lean hips and thighs, emphasising his maleness. Beneath the white shirt his powerful shoulder muscles moved in taut definition. She found that, somewhere along the line, she had forgotten to breathe and her gaze flickered away from the sardonic amusement in his eyes. He smelled of expensive aftershave, and danger—though she couldn't for the life of her have explained why.

'Sleep well?' he asked.

'Like a log, thanks.' She took several deep breaths, hoping he would put the sudden bright colour in her cheeks down to the hot coffee she had just swallowed. 'How's little Ben today?'

'I saw him about an hour ago.' He stifled a yawn. 'I think he's actually made a slight improvement.'

'Oh, that's wonderful news.'

'I'm not saying he's out of the woods yet, but it's the first positive piece of news we've had so far. With luck, we might even be thinking of sending him back to his village before too long.'

'You must be pleased.'

His dark brows drew together. 'I've learned from experience not to celebrate too soon.' His glance shifted to Greg. 'How's the clinic going?'

'Slowly.' Greg leaned back in his chair, stretching his arms above his head before sitting forward and kneading at his eyes. 'If progress so far is anything to go by, I could be stuck in Clinic for the rest of the afternoon. We seem to have a particularly heavy crop of expectant mums. They're all due to produce within the next couple of weeks.' He looked at Sam. 'I'd feel happier if I could see them all.'

'*Damn!*' Frowning, Sam ran a hand through his hair. 'I was hoping to get out to Mkesi. The clinic visit is well overdue and we're behind with the vaccination programme. Are you sure you couldn't hurry things up a bit?'

Greg looked doubtful. 'Not likely. One or two are presenting with possible complications. Could you get half the vaccinations done today and finish the rest next month?'

'I'd rather get it all over and done with.' Sam's dark brow furrowed. 'I've had word there's a particularly bad measles epidemic up north, and you know how fast these things can travel. Besides, it's unsettling for the children. No,' he shook his head. 'It needs two of us.'

He looked at Greg who raised his hands, drained his coffee and rose to his feet.

'Sorry, no can do. I'm due in Theatre in half an hour, then straight back to finish the clinic. Why not take Kate? You've finished your clinic, haven't you?'

She nodded, looking uncertainly from one to the other. 'I'd like to help if I can.'

Sam's face was drawn into a frown. 'I don't think it's a good idea.'

'She'll need to get to know the routine sooner or later. Why not start now?'

Kate drew a deep breath. 'What and where exactly is Mkesi?'

'It's one of the larger settlements,' Greg said. 'We usually do a routine monthly visit. It's quite an experience. You'd probably enjoy it.'

The sudden set of Sam's mouth suggested that he wasn't at all happy with the way things were going. 'It's not quite that simple. . .'

'Oh, come on, Sam. Give the girl a chance. You said yourself we all need to be able to adapt; take over for each other when necessary. What better time to start?'

Kate felt the dull colour rising in her cheeks. He doesn't want me with him, the thought echoed inside her head, filling her with an illogical sense of disappointment. Ridiculously, tears swam into her eyes. So, in spite of everything, he still thought of her as a liability. She blinked rapidly, setting her cup down.

'Yes, well, any time I *can* be useful, just let me know.'

'It's not that I don't think you're capable.' Sam's voice was curt, the message in his eyes all too clear. 'The fact is that it's a pretty long stint. Apart from that, it's taken a while to get these people to accept our presence at all. The children especially like what is familiar.'

'I can understand that.' With an effort she managed to keep her voice cool. 'Still, as I say, some other time, maybe. I'm sure I can find more than enough to keep me busy.'

A spasm flickered across his features, leaving them taut. 'This isn't personal.'

'No.' Her chin rose as she faced him. You just don't think I can handle it, she thought and how could she prove otherwise if she was never to be given the opportunity?

He was frowning, a deep cleft between the dark brows. 'On the other hand, maybe Greg is right. It would be good experience and I do need the help.' He looked at his watch. 'You'd better collect some gear and get yourself organised. We need extra packs of syringes, vaccines, broad-spectrum antibiotics. Oh, and, by the way, borrow a hat if you don't have one, and wear trousers. We leave in an hour and there's a lot of ground to cover if we're going to get back before dark.'

'Right.' She smiled, suppressing a tiny feeling of excitement. 'And thank. . .' But he was already striding away. 'Yes, sir; no, sir; three bags full, *sir*,' she muttered fiercely beneath her breath. What was it going to take? she wondered, to prove to Sam Brady that she was just as capable as the next man—or woman?

She was vaguely aware of the others drifting away and thought she was alone until Greg handed her a glass of fruit juice.

'Here, drink this and take a few deep breaths. It might

help. He doesn't mean anything by it, you know.'

Kate blinked hard. 'I'm sorry?'

'Don't take it to heart. It's just Sam being Sam. It's the way he is. His bark is worse than his bite.'

'I'll take your word for it.'

He laughed. 'He's all right, once you get to know him.'

She gave a crooked smile, her hands tightening round the glass she was holding. 'I should live so long.'

'Hey, come on. Don't take it too seriously. Sam carries a lot of responsibility. He's probably worried that you're doing too much too soon. It takes time to get properly acclimatised.'

A derisive smile tugged at her lips. 'On his side, are you?'

He grinned. 'Just don't tell him. I figure the less he knows, the better.' More seriously, he said, 'The job's not easy. I don't envy him the responsibility.'

'No, I don't imagine it is.' Kate felt her heart give an extra thud. 'I. . .I suppose it must be hard on his wife and family too.'

Greg looked at her with amused eyes. 'Now that you mention it, I did hear that Sara had very strong views on the subject.'

A large, suffocating cloud seemed suddenly to loom over Kate's head. Sam was married!

Even though she had told herself that it had to be so—that a man like Sam Brady had to have a woman in his life—the sense of shock hit her like a physical blow. She gave a tight smile. 'I imagine it must make periods of leave even more special. More couples do have to work apart these days. I don't suppose it's ever easy to adjust.'

Greg gave a hoot of laughter. 'I never met the lady, but I get the distinct impression that she wouldn't have shared your views.'

Kate stared at him, feeling the cloud shift slightly. 'I don't understand. You mean. . .'

'I don't know the gory details. George mentioned it in passing shortly before he went back to England. I just gathered that Sara wasn't the type to sit at home pining. The gist of it was that Sam managed to wangle some unexpected leave and went home, only to find that she'd packed up and gone. They were divorced about six months later, or so I heard.'

Kate swallowed hard as a dizzying and totally illogi- cal wave of relief swam through her. It lasted only as long as it took to bring her breathing back under control. All right, so Sam was divorced. As far as the law was concerned, he was free. But he was hardly likely to want to run the risk of getting involved again, was he? Even if she was interested—which she was not.

The heat was unbearable, rising in shimmering waves from the rough track that passed for a road. Nothing had prepared Kate as she clung to the open window of the truck, steadying herself and stifling a grunt each time they hit a rut.

Sam glanced briefly in her direction. She saw his mouth twitch. 'All right?'

'Absolutely.' She threw him a malevolent look as she nursed a tender spot on her elbow. At this rate, by the time they got to Mkesi she would be black and blue and he was enjoying himself enormously at her expense!

Gritting her teeth, she clung on. 'You said this was a routine visit?'

'Greg and I try to get out to most of the outlying villages or settlements once a month. We hold a clinic and generally deal with any problems that might have cropped up.'

'And what if there's an emergency in the meantime?'

'They get a message to us. Some can reach us by radio.'

'But what if you need to carry out surgery? There must be risks. Africa isn't your average British town.'

He glanced briefly in her direction. 'We do the best we can. It's not a perfect world. If it was, we wouldn't be here. Everyone knows the dangers and takes care to avoid them.'

Sensible people, she thought, deliberately settling herself as far from the lean, masculine frame as the restricted confines of the vehicle allowed. Even so, the smell of expensive aftershave drifted into her nostrils. Dressed in faded jeans, the material stretched taut against the hard muscles of his thighs, Sam Brady looked powerfully masculine.

She let her gaze drift idly in his direction. It seemed unfair that anyone could look so cool, so unruffled, in such heat. He stared straight ahead, concentrating on keeping the vehicle on the road, allowing her a clear view of his profile.

He turned to look directly at her and for several seconds Kate stared into the thickly lashed blue eyes which, at this moment were filled with sardonic amusement as, lazily, he reached out a muscular arm. She stiffened, feeling the breath catch in her throat.

A glimmer of amusement flickered in his eyes as he brushed away a fly that had become tangled in her hair before turning his gaze back to the road ahead. 'Naughty, naughty, Dr Stewart. You didn't remember to use your insect repellent.'

With a quick intake of breath she looked away, conscious of the warm colour tinging her cheeks. It was a relief when, some time later, he pointed ahead. 'That's the settlement. We should be there in about five minutes.'

She felt a tremor of excitement run through her

as she strained her eyes to see what it was that he wanted her to see—her first glimpse of a village. And then, suddenly, it was there—a large clearing circled by trees, framed against the distant hills of the Great Rift Valley.

CHAPTER FIVE

SAM grinned. 'It looks as if the reception committee is out in force.'

Within seconds, as the tyres crunched to a halt in the dust, they were surrounded by children of all ages and sizes, waving and laughing, hands reaching in to tug at their hands and clothes.

'Hey, Ntanin, you've grown.' Sam was climbing out of the Land Rover to clasp a young teenager by the hand.

Kate scrambled out after him. The smiling faces crowded in, small children climbed in and over the vehicle, grinning shyly as they stared at her with wide brown eyes.

'Hello.' She smiled down at a child who couldn't have been more than six, who shyly pushed a small fist into her own hand and clung to her. Bending down, Kate smiled. 'And what's your name?'

'That's Daniel.'

She glanced up to see Sam striding towards her. He was carrying a child on his shoulders, her plump little hands clinging to his dark hair as she squealed with laughter.

'Come on, we'd better unload and get the medical stuff set up. The sooner we get started the sooner we'll be able to get back.' He slid the child to the ground, kissing her on the nose and murmuring something that drew a shy giggle from her before she ran off to join her friends.

Kate looked at him, grinning. 'What's this, then—favouritism?'

'You could say that.' His blue eyes darkened compassionately. 'Much as you fight against it, there's often one case that gets to you. Suzi is a special case. You may not guess it to look at her, but she's HIV positive. Her father died of Aids about six months ago. Her mother probably won't make it through to the next harvest, and Suzi. . .' His mouth compressed. 'I'm sure I don't need to spell it out.'

Kate frowned. 'I suppose the problem is on the increase?'

He handed her one of the boxes. 'I was going to say you get used to it. That's not true. You deal with it. Sometimes you just have to learn to switch off, otherwise you'd be no use to anyone.'

'But Suzi looks so happy, so. . .so well.'

'That's the nature of the disease. As long as we can keep her that way we will. But it's no good fooling ourselves. Recovery isn't on the agenda, not where Suzi is concerned.' He straightened up, hoisting one of the boxes onto his shoulder. 'Come on, we've got work to do. I could give you a blow by blow account of each patient, but I think it's probably better if we just take each case as it comes.'

For no reason Kate could have explained, that simple inclusion of herself felt very satisfying.

'We'll set up by one of those huts over there. At least it will give us a bit of shade to work in.'

She followed, seeing him smile and pause to talk to the villagers who clearly welcomed him in their midst, and the thought occurred to her that he belonged here; that this was his element.

She gave a rueful smile as they moved on between the groups of small round huts. 'You obviously don't have any trouble communicating. I'm not sure my use of sign language is going to have quite the desired effect. How am I going to communicate, Sam? There are limits even to my ingenuity.'

He grinned, beckoning one of the younger women

who had been watching them shyly. 'This is Mary Oleit. She is sixteen and speaks some English. Mary would like to go to the city one day to train as a nurse.' He smiled at the girl. 'Mary, this is Dr Stewart.'

The girl smiled. 'Doctor.'

'Well, we can certainly do with all the good nurses we can get. Hello, Mary. I shall be glad of your help. It looks as if we're in for a busy day, so the sooner we get started the better.'

Watched by a group of naked and totally uninhibited children, Kate unfolded the small table and set it up in the shade. Her movements were purely mechanical as she laid out the supplies. She checked boxes of pain-killing tablets, dressings, vitamin supplements and antibiotics carefully into a large tray and, after a moment's hesitation, surreptitiously added a packet of brightly coloured sweets she had slipped into her bag at the last minute.

Sam's mouth quirked. 'What's this, then—bribery and corruption, Dr Stewart?'

'A few sweets never hurt anyone, provided they're in moderation of course. Besides,' she put in determinedly, 'most of the children have probably never tasted a piece of chocolate in their lives. Why should they be denied a simple pleasure? Or are you going to tell me it's against the rules?'

For a second a nerve pulsed in his jaw and she thought he was angry. Then he gave a sheepish grin and, fumbling in his pocket, he produced another packet.

'Liquorice Allsorts,' he muttered. 'It just so happens I'm rather partial to them myself.'

Their eyes met and they both grinned. It was a revelation, Kate thought, as she revelled in her first long look at Sam Brady. Seeing him this close, this relaxed, she was acutely aware of his lean, muscled body, the firm but sensuous mouth and square jaw.

There was a quiet strength about him, not entirely

physical, the kind that made him always a natural leader. The kind of man whom others would be glad to follow. She wondered if he was aware of it and the kind of power it gave him and suddenly, illogically, she found herself envying any woman who was part of his life.

She dragged her thoughts back quickly to safer ground and the queue that had already begun to form in front of them. Within minutes, Kate was smiling reassuringly at her first patient.

The boy aged, Kate guessed, about fourteen, limped forward to sit awkwardly in the chair provided. He was tall and wore the *shuka*, a cotton cloth worn as a cloak, across his body and tied at the shoulder.

He thrust one leg forward, exposing a large ulcer, and she couldn't help feeling a twinge of sympathy for the youth as he sat, blinking hard, while Kate tried, as gently as possible, to inspect the affected area.

The bleb had obviously recently ruptured, oozing out a grey-green slough which had spread to the surrounding tissue. The edges of the ulcer were raised and looked raw and Kate felt him tense as her surgically gloved fingers strayed too close.

Smiling sympathetically, she straightened up. 'I'm sorry; I didn't mean to hurt you.'

'Not hurt.' His mouth trembled slightly.

'No.' It wasn't true but she respected his need to maintain a façade of bravery in front of the waiting onlookers. 'Did you injure your leg before the ulcer appeared?'

He shrugged. 'Maybe.'

'Not getting much help?'

Stifling a sigh, she glanced up to meet Sam's gaze and gave a slight smile. 'Not a lot.'

He continued with the dressing he was working on, glancing at the ulcer. 'It looks nasty.'

'Yes, I know.' She peered at it again, carefully swabbing the affected area. 'But at least it looks as if the damage is limited to the superficial fascia—none of the tendons or blood vessels seem to be affected.'

'Probably football.'

She looked at Sam. 'I'm sorry?'

'Football.' His mouth twitched. 'It's the favourite game. Things tend to get a little over-heated.'

'Ah,' she grinned. 'Well, I always like to know what I'm dealing with. It makes life a lot easier.' Having cleaned the ulcer with hypertonic magnesium sulphate, she reached for a bottle, dispensing procaine penicillin tablets into a bottle and handing them to the youth.

'You must take these tablets three times a day,' she emphasised. 'They will help the ulcer to heal and you must keep it clean. Keep the dressing on until,' she called after the retreating child, 'the skin has healed. Oh, well,' she smiled wryly. 'It's nice to be appreciated.'

More than once during that afternoon, as she worked her way through the steady procession of patients, she had reason to be grateful to Mary Oleit, who acted both as assistant and interpreter.

Kate wiped a droplet of sweat from her eyes, feeling the dust and perspiration on her skin and lips as she examined her next patient.

The child sitting on the makeshift examination couch was aged about six, but looked less. As Mary passed her the stethoscope and Kate listened to the small chest, she felt her throat tighten as the child gazed up at her with eyes which had a curious smoky appearance, wiping a hand across her runny nose.

Easing her back, Kate managed, with an effort, to smile. 'She's not in very good shape, is she?'

Mary Oleit shook her head. 'This little one came to Mkesi two weeks ago. She was very poorly.'

'Yes, I can believe it,' Kate frowned. 'She's very underweight.' Gently she pinched the child's paper-like skin. 'Where are her parents?'

'We don't know. She was brought to the village by

her uncle whose sister lives here. He took the child when the mother died and the father was forced to go to the town to find work. He said he would be back but. . .' She shrugged. 'It happens. The uncle said he couldn't keep a child who couldn't see.' Her hands rose expressively. 'She is no use to him, you see.'

Stifling a feeling of anger, Kate reached for her ophthalmoscope to examine the child's eyes. Biting at her lip, she studied the tiny white, sticky, foam-like spots on the conjunctiva. Both eyes were affected, causing the whites of the eyes to become dry and rough-looking. She straightened up as Sam spoke.

'Mind if I take a look?'

'Be my guest.' She moved aside, flexing her arms wearily. 'In fact, I'd be grateful for your opinion. I think I've read about this condition but it's not something I've ever come across until now.'

He leaned forward and began, gently, to make his own examination before turning to her again.

'I haven't seen too many cases like this myself, but I'd say it's xerophthalmia—dry eye disease. Most common in places like India and Indonesia, where the diet consists mainly of rice or white maize or other vitamin-deficient staples. But you do get a few cases here in Africa and in Latin America too.'

Kate looked at him. 'So it's primarily caused by vitamin deficiency?'

Sam nodded. 'Specifically vitamin A. That, and a generally poor standard of living.' His mouth twisted. 'This isn't your rich man's disease, and breast-fed babies aren't likely to be affected. It starts once the baby is weaned onto a diet consisting of little more than rice or gruel.'

Kate brushed the back of her hand across her forehead. 'So what do you suggest, apart from the obvious—a better diet, eggs, milk, fish?'

His blue eyes narrowed. 'The bonus is that it's been

recognised in time. If it hadn't been, the cornea would eventually have ruptured, causing blindness.'

'Obviously we'll need to get her started on doses of vitamin A.'

'Give it by mouth rather than injection.' And added, when she raised a questioning eyebrow, 'Two hundred thousand international units given by mouth on two days successively will be more effective and more practical, unless you're planning on staying overnight. This way we can leave the appropriate dosage with a responsible adult. She'll need a third dose in about two weeks' time. Hopefully that, and a change in diet, should do the trick—for this little one anyway.'

'Thanks a lot.' Kate's eyes flashed her gratitude.

'Glad to be of help.'

He ran a hand over the child's curly hair and she watched as, grinning, Sam finished his examination of a lively five-year-old before kissing the top of her head and setting her down on her feet.

'She's doing very well,' he told the anxiously waiting mother, who seemed little more than eighteen years old herself. 'Keep giving her the antibiotics. The ulcer is healing nicely. Here, better not forget this.'

Kate watched, fascinated, as, smiling shyly, the child reached for a pair of crutches, but it was only as they moved away across the open compound that she realised with a sense of shock that the child was dragging one stick-like leg.

She looked up to find Sam watching her. She moistened her dry lips with her tongue. 'Polio?'

He nodded grimly. 'She's one of the lucky ones. I've seen worse. I was out in India briefly. I saw kiddies who could only get about on all fours, like little animals, and the hellish thing is that one simple vaccination could have prevented it.'

She looked at him and swallowed hard. 'Whatever

we do it's like one drop in a huge ocean. It all seems so futile.'

'I don't agree. Things *are* changing. It may take another ten years, twenty—who knows? But the message will get through. It doesn't have to be like this.'

'I wish I had your optimism,' she said raggedly.

'You're tired, that's all. Why not take a break? You've earned it. We've been working pretty steadily since we arrived.'

She shook her head and immediately wished she hadn't as a wave of dizziness hit her. Almost without being aware of it, she brushed a hand weakly against her forehead.

He was instantly concerned. 'Are you all right?'

'What?' She moistened her dry lips. 'Oh. . . Yes. I'm fine. I just felt a little dizzy for a few seconds, that's all. It must be the heat.'

The thought of standing under a cold shower rose tantalisingly in her mind and was pushed hurriedly away as she became aware of him staring down at her, his gaze roaming over her flushed cheeks. At least she told herself it was the heat. His nearness was oddly unnerving.

'It's nothing. I'd rather press on.'

'The rest can wait.' His voice was surprisingly concerned. 'You've been working at full stretch since you arrived and you still haven't had a chance to acclimatise. There's a flask of juice in the truck. Why not go and have a drink? Relax for a while. I'll finish up here.'

'There's no need for that.' Her lips trembled. 'I'm fine. Besides, the sooner we finish the sooner we can get back.'

Humour glinted briefly in his blue eyes. 'And the sooner you can get away from me—is that it? Am I really such an ogre?'

She flashed him a look. 'I didn't say that.'

'You didn't have to—you have an amazingly expressive face, Dr Stewart.'

She swallowed hard, feeling strangely at odds with herself. What was it about this man that he seemed to have such an unsettling effect on her? 'I'd really rather carry on. We're nearly finished, anyway.'

With a quick movement she turned away, licking her dry lips. Her hands were shaking as she began to clear away the used equipment and, to her dismay, one of the instruments slipped from her grasp. Without thinking, she moved to catch it, gasping as the razor-sharp steel cut into the fleshy palm of her hand.

It was only a small cut but the blood welled up and instinctively she clenched her hand, closing her eyes.

Sam was instantly concerned. 'Let me see,' he said in a quietly controlled voice.

She shook her head. 'It's just a small cut, that's all. It'll be fine.' She made to turn away but Sam's hand came down on her arm, forcing her to unclench her fingers.

He gazed at the wound and swore softly under his breath. 'It'll need cleaning properly with antiseptic.'

'I'll see to it when I've cleared these things away.'

His mouth took on an ominously angry look. 'You crazy little fool. Surely you, of all people, must know that if it's not dealt with straight away even the smallest cut or injury can become infected. Don't *ever* ignore something like this, no matter how minor it might seem.'

He reached for a swab, soaking it with antiseptic and began, gently, to cleanse the wound.

The cool touch of his hand on her flesh was utterly unexpected and startlingly intimate as his fingers brushed against her palm.

Shock brought a warm tide of colour flooding into her cheeks but, once the initial moment of shock had faded, there was no denying that it was a disconcertingly pleasurable experience, Kate thought as she closed her eyes and opened them again to encounter the familiar dark shape of his head only inches away.

He straightened up. 'I think that's clean. I'll put a small dressing on it for now, but I want you to get it checked just to be sure there's no infection. That's an order.'

Resentment flared briefly. 'Has anyone ever told you you're a bully, Dr Brady?' she muttered.

A nerve pulsed in his jaw. 'Frequently. It goes with the territory. I can live with that.'

She could believe it. Blue eyes met hers and Kate swallowed hard on the sudden tightness in her throat. Her nostrils were filled with the warm, male scent of him, teasing her senses and filling her with confusion. This shouldn't be happening. She felt dazed by her reaction to a man she scarcely knew—didn't want to know.

They stared into each other's eyes. She saw him tense and was totally unprepared as his hand rose suddenly to graze the soft fullness of her mouth. It was feather-light, totally unexpected, and it made her blood pound through her veins, leaving her breathless and light-headed as he slowly bent his head and the sensuous mouth moved closer.

She sensed a tautening of his muscles, heard his sharp intake of breath and found herself watching in rapt fascination as his face loomed closer. For an instant she resisted, then his lips brushed against hers, softly, unhurriedly. He cupped her face in his hands, moaning softly as he drew her slowly towards him.

'No, I. . .' Kate strained backwards, her hands against his chest as she tried to push him away. This shouldn't be happening.

She gasped as his fingers linked with hers, turning them to expose her open palm. She tried to snatch her hand from his grasp but frustratingly his grip merely tightened, sending a tingling awareness surging through her as he stared at the third finger of her left hand.

'I can't believe some man hasn't wanted to put a ring there.' She tensed and saw him frown. 'There was someone?'

She swallowed hard, managing with an effort to keep her voice calm. 'I thought so, for a while.'

A brief hardness flared in his eyes. 'What happened?'

'I'm. . .still not sure.'

'So why did you leave him?'

She gave a slight laugh. It sounded oddly breathless. 'What makes you think I did?'

'Because no man in his right mind would let you go.'

'Unless, of course, he found someone else.' Suddenly she was having difficulty swallowing.

'So what happened?'

'We worked together.' She was surprised to hear herself talking quite calmly. 'We shared the same group of friends; went everywhere together. I suppose it was more or less inevitable that people began to think of us as a couple.'

Sam's mouth tightened, a nerve pulsing in his jaw. 'What went wrong?'

She stiffened as his persistent probing began to stir memories she would have preferred to remain buried. 'I suppose I just didn't see what was happening.' Suddenly weary, she raked a hand through her hair, lifting its weight from her neck. 'Maybe I was just too involved with my work. Maybe I should have had more time for the things that were important to Jeremy.'

She frowned. Why was she telling him all this? It had taken nine months of her life to bury it so completely that she thought it would never surface again. She drew a deep breath and looked at him directly. 'He found someone else. I can't blame him for that.' Her fingers clenched.

'Did you love him?' He released them slowly.

A slight shiver shook her frame, though it had nothing to do with being cold. 'Yes. No.' Resentment flared. 'I thought so at the time. Obviously I was mistaken. Maybe my pride was hurt.'

Sam's gentle fingers lifted her chin, and she felt the colour surge into her cheeks. 'The man's a fool. It wasn't your fault, Kate. You have to believe that. Holding on to the past doesn't change anything. Sometimes you just have to learn to let go.'

'You make it sound so easy.'

'It is easy. You just have to want it to happen.'

But was that what she wanted? She fought a rising sense of panic. She didn't know anything about this man, except that he seemed to represent everything that made her feel vulnerable.

His lips brushed against hers. She closed her eyes, her mouth dry with a nervousness that seemed to have no logic to it, then suddenly he tensed and she was free.

'We'd better get back,' he said huskily.

She nodded, confusion clouding her eyes as she battled with an inner sense of disappointment. What was happening to her? More to the point, why was she letting it happen? Hadn't she learned anything from the past?

It was only later, as she showered and climbed into bed, that she began to acknowledge that her feelings about Sam Brady were far too confused and definitely unprofessional, and she found the thought oddly troubling.

The fact that Sam had kissed her, held her in his arms, didn't mean a thing. He had been the injured party when his marriage broke up but that didn't mean that his feelings for the woman he had loved had been wiped out; that he didn't still care.

Kate sighed. Everything was happening too fast, getting out of control. She had come to Africa to forget about the past and to make a fresh start. The last thing she needed was a whole new set of complications, least of all a complication in the shape of Sam Brady.

CHAPTER SIX

DAYS should be longer, Kate thought as, having changed her blouse for the second time that morning, she made her way back to the children's ward.

More than a week of trying to avoid anything other than fleeting contact with Sam had proved more wearing than she would have believed possible, especially when it seemed that she had only to turn around and he was there.

Nor did the fact that she knew her reasoning was totally illogical make things any easier. *Blast the man!* she bridled defensively, scuttling away from the glimpse of the distant, white-coated figure and promptly heading in the opposite direction. Was it any wonder she felt exhausted?

On the ward, Jill greeted her arrival with a slightly harassed expression. 'Sorry to drop you straight in at the deep end, but we've had a couple of query admissions—one a possible skull fracture. Would you take a look?'

'Have we got the X-rays?' Kate was already following her, accepting the large buff envelope from which she extracted the film as they made for the small office. Sliding it onto the screen, she leaned forward to study it more closely. 'Hmm, well, there's certainly something there.' Frowning, she traced a faint line with her finger. 'Do we know what happened?'

'This is all we have.' Jill handed her the notes. 'It seems a fight broke out over some food. Things turned a bit nasty and the fists started flying.' She smiled wryly. 'We got the loser. Mind you, I'd hate to see the others!'

Kate grinned before turning her attention back to the screen. 'Well, we don't want to take any chances. Let's take a closer look.' She shifted the position of a small light. 'Yes, I'd say that's a fracture. Can you see it? A hairline.'

Jill nodded, straightening up. 'Do you want to keep him in?'

'Yes, best be on the safe side.' Unclipping her pen from the pocket of her blue shirt, Kate wrote up her notes. 'One thing's for sure, he's going to have the mother of all headaches for a couple of days.'

Jill pulled a face. 'These things flare up and get out of hand before you know it.' She slid the film back into its envelope. 'At least it might give tempers a chance to cool.'

'I'm not surprised tempers get frayed.' Kate glanced up from checking her notes, easing the shirt from her back. 'Keep an eye on him. Let me know if there's any change or if you're not happy about him.' She gave a slight smile. 'I should think what he'll need most is a good sleep, but I've written him up for painkillers if he needs them. Right, so who's next?'

Running a hand across her forehead, Kate followed as Jill made her way between the rows of metal-framed beds and found herself fighting a growing sense of frustration.

The wooden floor was scrubbed to a pristine cleanliness; curtains, which could be drawn between the beds, added a splash of colour. But by any standards the conditions were still primitive and there had been times, during the past couple of weeks, when she had been reduced almost to tears by the lack of even the most basic items of equipment—things she would have taken so much for granted back home.

Nothing of her feelings was evident, however, as they came to a halt at the side of the bed where a man sat hunched forward and wheezing breathlessly.

Joseph Evaliste was fifty years old. Tall and ebony-skinned, he was severely underweight. Clutching a hand to his chest, he produced a dry, rasping cough, leaving a tiny fleck of blood at the corner of his mouth.

Uncoiling her stethoscope, Kate spoke to Simon Mxoli, the orderly, who was filling a water jug. 'Will you ask him how long he's been like this, and explain to him that I need to examine him before I can help him?'

He questioned the man, listening carefully to his stumbling replies before looking at Kate. 'He says he has had the cough a long time.'

Kate frowned. Having listened to the low-pitched respirations and typical laboured breathing of a patient with chronic bronchitis, she dropped her stethoscope into her pocket.

'When he says "a long time", does he mean weeks, months. . .?' She waited for Simon to translate.

'He says many months. First not too bad, then more.' He listened as the man spoke, pressing a hand to his chest and drawing a deep breath. 'He says it is worse in the morning—very tight.'

'And does he cough anything up? Is there any blood? Is he always breathless?'

He spoke to the man again before nodding. 'He says yes.'

'Thank you.' Smiling reassuringly at her patient, Kate moved away from the bed slightly, frowning as she scanned the notes. 'Hmm, it's not looking too good, is it? It looks to me like a classic case of COADs—chronic obstruction of the airways disease.'

'What can you do?' Jill watched Simon Mxoli straightening the man's pillows.

Kate shook her head. 'Unfortunately there's not a lot we can do. We can't cure the condition, but at least we can treat the symptoms and try to make him more comfortable. First we need to treat the infection he's got bubbling away in there. The last thing we need is

for him to go into respiratory failure.' She took the
notes Jill proffered, glancing through them again before
handing them back.

'We'll start him on ampicillin, two hundred and fifty
milligrams twice a day for seven days to start. If the
cough troubles him at night we can try him on pholcod-
ine and steam inhalations. Let's keep a close eye on him
for the next few days, anyway, and see how he goes.'

She was writing up her notes when Tessa Dioulu
entered the ward. Aged about twenty-five, she was slim
and wore her white uniform with its mauve belt with
pride. Born in Ghana, her parents had moved to Britain
where her father was an orthopaedic specialist. Her face
was anxious as she spoke quietly to Jill.

Kate closed the buff folder, dropping it onto the trolley before looking up. 'Problems?'

Jill nodded, frowning. 'We're a bit worried about
one of the children. Her mother brought her to the
out-patients' clinic a couple of days ago. Sam examined
her and decided she should be admitted straight away.'

'I'd better take a look at her.' Kate looked at Tessa.
'Do you know what the symptoms were?'

Quietly efficient, the girl matched her steps to Kate's
as she led the way to the children's ward. Her pretty
face, with its high cheek-bones, was anxious. 'Severe
headache, persistent high-pitched crying, fever.'

Kate shot her a look. 'Any rash?'

The girl nodded and Kate's mouth tightened.

The door to the ward swung open beneath the gentle
pressure of Jill's hand. 'Her name is Bibesa. We've put
her in the side ward because of the possible risk of
cross-infection. She's in here.'

They each donned a surgical mask and gown before
entering the small side ward.

The child, who couldn't be more than about three
years of age, lay in one of the metal-framed cots. Her

tiny, splayed limbs were dewed with sweat and she moved restlessly in her sleep.

'Sam wanted her kept deeply sedated to restrict her movements.' Jill looked at Kate. 'One of the village children died a couple of weeks ago of meningitis.'

Kate felt her heart give a dull thud as she reached automatically for the notes, flipping the page and biting at her lower lip. 'I see she's on chloramphenicol.'

Tessa nodded, her brow furrowing above her mask as she checked the infant's pulse. 'Her blood pressure started dropping about half an hour ago.'

Kate reached down to press her hand gently to the child's warm, flushed skin. Straightening up, she said, 'What's her temperature?'

Jill shook down the thermometer. 'Forty centigrade.' She made a careful note of the reading before looking up, her eyes troubled. 'It's not looking good, is it?'

'It's certainly confusing.' Kate frowned. 'Have you tried to get hold of Sam?'

'He's still in Theatre.'

'*Damn!*' She drew a breath, taking in the child's restlessness before her gaze shifted again to the monitor above the bed. 'I don't think this is going to wait for Sam. I need to examine her properly,' she said decisively.

'What do you think is wrong?'

'I'm not sure yet, but I aim to find out.' Uncoiling her stethoscope, she listened, frowning, to the child's rapid heartbeat before straightening up. 'I take it Sam did a lumbar puncture?'

'Yes, the results have just come through.' Jill handed her the lab report.

Kate scanned it, biting at her lower lip. 'According to this, the protein level is normal.' She flipped the page. 'So is the sugar level.'

'Is that a problem?'

Tugging down her mask, Kate drew a deep breath.

'If it *is* meningitis we're dealing with I would have expected the protein level to be raised and the sugar level to be low. According to this, neither is the case. What we do seem to have is evidence of pus.'

Jill looked at her, frowning. 'Which means what?'

'I'd say we're not looking at meningitis here. We have something else.' She frowned. 'My guess would be septicaemia. 'Glancing through the lab report, she tapped the page. 'I see from the notes there was some mention of a sore throat before she became feverish and developed the other, more serious symptoms.'

Jill released a slow breath. 'So what do you want to do?'

'Is there any history of allergic reaction to penicillin?'

'Not that we know of.'

'In that case, I want to give her an immediate intramuscular injection of benzathine penicillin. The sooner we can get her fever down the better. Apart from that there's not a lot we can do, other than making sure she has plenty of fluids.'

Kate drew up the injection, administering it quickly and efficiently, only vaguely aware of the door quietly swinging open. 'There we are. Hopefully that should do the trick. With any luck we should know one way or the other within the next couple of hours.'

Suddenly she felt drained. Using her forearm to wipe away the thin film of sweat from her forehead, she looked up and saw Sam. His blue eyes met and held hers. He looked tired. She could see the perspiration dotting the fine pores of his bronzed skin and the taut line of his jaw, and knew a sudden, primitive urge to reach out and touch him.

'What the hell is going on here?'

She froze in the act of dropping the syringe into the steel dish Jill was holding ready. She couldn't believe she had heard the words. Her glance flew up to meet his and she was shocked by the anger she saw in his eyes.

'I asked a question.'

Before she could begin to explain, the child moved, stirring restlessly. Sam's gaze swung in her direction and back to Kate's pale face as, dizzily, she stripped off her surgical gloves and loosened her mask.

'I'll take over now,' he said, brusquely. 'I suggest you go outside and get some air. I'll talk to you later.'

She went without looking back, stripping off her gown and flinging it with her gloves and mask into the bin. Like an automaton she walked through the ward. The swing door opened beneath the pressure of her hand as she made her way blindly out into the cooling evening air, her hands gripping the rail of the veranda as she willed herself to breathe evenly.

In the distance, the lights from small camp fires dotted the darkness. A smell of cooking wafted across the night air, filling her nostrils. She had been hungry but suddenly her appetite seemed to have deserted her.

'*Damn you*, Sam Brady.' Tears swam into her eyes. She blinked them away rapidly. Clearly nothing had changed. He still didn't trust her. How could she have been so naïve as to think that it might have done?

Making her way down the steps, she wended her way across the compound. Leaning her back against one of the trees, she stared up at the clear, star-filled sky and, for some reason, found that it evoked memories of home and of Jeremy—filling her with a sense of homesickness.

In a gesture of frustration she brushed angrily at the tear which rolled down her cheek. Why now? Just when she had imagined that she was beginning to get her feelings so well under control at last. How could she have forgotten so soon what it was like to be lulled into a false sense of security?

If nothing else, hadn't she learned from her experience with Jeremy that all the sweet words and promises in the world only led to a fool's paradise? She thought she had learned her lesson, but she was wrong. The realisation that she was still vulnerable hit her with the force of a shock wave and she sniffed hard, then gasped as a tall figure moved quietly out of the shadows towards her.

'Sulking, Kate?'

'Sam!' she exclaimed, panic giving way to relief and some other emotion which she adamantly refused to put a name to. She furiously blinked the tears away from her eyes, conscious, yet again of the inexplicable feeling of sheer physical attraction she always felt whenever he came near. She dashed a hand across her eyes as he came to a halt in front of her. 'Do you have to creep like that?'

'I wasn't creeping,' he drawled softly. 'You just weren't listening.'

'I was taking your advice. I needed some fresh air,' she said thickly. 'It's been a long day, so if you don't mind. . .'

'Kate, don't go. At least not until we've talked.' His hands came down on her shoulders. He looked tired, she realised. Lines of exhaustion were etched around his eyes and mouth.

'There's nothing to say.' She drew a long breath. 'I really am tired. . .' She half turned away but, infuriatingly, his grip merely tightened. She didn't want to talk. Just to be near him was enough to set the alarm bells ringing in her brain. She stiffened, her face taut with strain as she tried to pull away.

'At least let me say what I have to say.'

'Oh, I think you've already said more than enough, Dr Brady, don't you?'

His face darkened. 'I think I owe you an apology.'

Shocked, she stopped in her tracks, turning to look at him. 'Yes, now that you come to mention it, I think you do,' she flared. 'You questioned my professional judgement—again.'

He gave a slight laugh. 'Funny, for a while there I thought the boot was on the other foot.'

'I don't know what you mean. I wouldn't do that.'

'Not even if it was justified?' he said, softly.

She stared at him. 'But it isn't...wasn't. That wasn't...'

'Kate, I was treating a child for the symptoms of meningitis.' He raked a hand through his hair, leaving a tuft standing on end. For some reason it made him seem oddly vulnerable and it needed an effort of will not to go to him—to smooth it down.

She drew herself up sharply. 'Oh, come on, Sam. You're tired. We both are. We don't need to get into this...'

'I made a wrong diagnosis.'

She stared at him. 'Under the given circumstances you had no choice. You treated the symptoms as you saw them at the time. I would have come to the same conclusions.' Without thinking, she had moved closer, involuntarily resting her hand on his arm. 'Sam, you were right to do what you did.'

She felt the muscles beneath her fingers tense. His face was taut. 'I made a mistake. You were right. I want to thank you for what you did.'

'Oh, come on, Sam. You're not making any kind of sense. When you first saw the child you had every reason to draw the conclusion you did. If there was any doubt at all about the diagnosis you had to take the necessary precautionary measures. You did what any doctor would have done.'

'You think so.' He looked down at her hand and, as if suddenly becoming aware of what she was doing, she withdrew it quickly, feeling the warm colour flood into her cheeks.

She stiffened. 'In spite of what you might think, I wasn't questioning your judgement. The symptoms had developed since the child was admitted. Her blood pressure had started to fall. *I* had the benefit of the results of the tests *you* ordered. I was only doing what you would have done if you had been there. That's all there was to it. And now, if you don't mind, I really am tired. . .'

'Kate.' His face darkened. She had half turned away but infuriatingly his grip merely tightened, turning her to face him. His touch sent a shock wave darting through her. She took a deep breath, her face taut with strain. 'I'm sorry if you thought I seemed to doubt you.'

She stiffened, trying to pull away—trying to re-establish the mental safety barriers between them. 'Let's just forget it, shall we? It's not important.'

'I think it is.' He drew a hand wearily across his forehead and his voice tightened. 'I came out of Theatre to be told there was an emergency. I got to the ward to find you treating one of my patients.' He drew a breath. 'The truth is that my anger wasn't directed at you—it was directed at what I thought was my own misjudgement.'

Her gaze levelled with his. 'In the early stages anyone could mistake the symptoms of meningitis for those of septicaemia, especially when, as in this case, there was known contact with a previous case of meningitis.'

'I know that now.' His mouth twisted. 'I over-reacted. I'm sorry. I just wanted to set the record straight, that's all.'

The admission left her feeling winded. They stood facing each other, yet the tension sparking between them suddenly had nothing to do with anger. It was something far more subtle. She could feel the pulse hammering in her throat as she faced him.

Her gaze was drawn to the sensuous mouth and the dark eyes, which seemed to be drawing her out of her depth. His tautly muscled body was so close that she could feel the beat of his heart against the reckless tumult of her own. The breath snagged in her throat.

She was totally unprepared for his touch as slowly he bent his head towards her, one finger lazily tracing the sweet fullness of her mouth. The lazy brush of his mouth against her own set her pulses racing. It was a feather-light caress, yet it left her feeling breathless and light-headed, suffusing her body with heat.

'You must know I want you,' he murmured huskily.

His kiss, a powerful but subtle invasion of her mouth, made her gasp as he tasted the tender curve of her lips. Vaguely she was aware that his fingers were stroking, moving gently, with infinite care.

Of course she knew—how could she not know? She trembled beneath his touch, shaken by her unbidden response to him. He was making her feel alive in a way she had never been before—heightening her senses, making her experience sensations in a way that was both new and exciting and frightening all at once.

He raised his head briefly to look at her. He groaned softly as his mouth resumed its teasing foray, drawing her ever deeper.

Her breath caught in her throat. Desire threatened to flare out of control and, with that awareness, another new realisation came homing in to her bemused senses. If she wasn't very careful there was every danger of her becoming seriously attracted to Sam Brady.

Confused, she lifted her face to his, a new awareness bringing the colour to her cheeks. She could hear the muted sound of her own heartbeat as his mouth claimed hers again, cutting off the protest that rose fleetingly to her lips. It would be so easy to let go; to allow herself to be caught up; to be seduced by the things he seemed to be offering. But that was the very thing that made him dangerous. The warning echoed through her head, filling her with turmoil.

This was crazy—she had to stop it now, while there was still time. 'No!' In desperation she dragged her mouth away from the delicious torment he was inflicting. Don't get involved, a warning voice rang deep inside her brain. You're here to do a job—get on with it as unemotionally as possible.

Unfortunately, where Sam was concerned, that was always going to be far easier said than done.

CHAPTER SEVEN

IT WAS seven-thirty in the morning but, if anything, the heat was even more intense than usual as Kate checked her appearance in the mirror, seeing the full denim skirt and the neat, white, short-sleeved blouse. Her hair, still damp from the shower, was held back in a French plait, keeping its weight from her neck. Even so, she didn't fool herself. Five minutes from now she would be bathed in sweat again.

Crossing to the ward, she smiled a greeting at the group of waiting women who sat with their babies in one of the few patches of shade beneath a clump of trees.

For the past three weeks storm clouds had been gathering and the air had become ominously heavy. During the night she had even heard the occasional rumble of thunder but there was still no sign of rain. It was as if nature had decided deliberately to be perverse, Kate thought as, with a sigh, she ran lightly up the steps and, shrugging herself into her white coat, made her way to the ward.

The day's routine, under the gently efficient guidance of Sister Julie Lyongi, was already well under way as Kate headed for the small side ward.

Catching sight of her, Julie, tall and attractive in the crisp white uniform, quickly handed the dish she was holding to one of the orderlies and anxiously came to greet her.

'Dr Stewart, I am so sorry, I was not expecting. . .'

'It's all right.' Kate was quick to offer the smiling reassurance. She lowered her voice conspiratorially. 'I shouldn't be here. I'm supposed to be taking a clinic, but I just had to pop in to see how little Bibesa is doing.'

'Ah, yes.' The girl smiled as she led the way to the small side ward. 'She seems a little better this morning. She was restless during the night, but that was to be expected. She took a little water a while ago and began to sleep more easily.'

'Oh, that's wonderful news.'

'Would you like me to bring you the notes?'

'Oh, no.' Kate gave a slight laugh. 'As I said, officially I shouldn't be here but perhaps I'll just pop in and have a quick look at her, if that's all right?'

'Please.' Julie smiled, indicating the door. 'If you need me I will be giving out the medication.' She sped gracefully away, leaving Kate to slip quietly into the room.

Gazing down at the small child lying in the cot, Kate felt a surge of relief as she saw for herself that the child was indeed breathing more easily. Pressing the back of her hand lightly against the baby's flesh, it was gratifying to discover, too, that it was no longer clammy— that the worst of the fever had gone and the tiny limbs were more relaxed.

Swallowing hard on the sudden tightness in her throat, she rested her arms on the cot rails and smiled. 'I think you're going to be just fine, sweetheart. Well done.'

'I had a feeling I might find you in here.'

Sam spoke from the doorway. He was carrying his white coat slung over one shoulder, revealing his tautly muscled arms and chest beneath a black T-shirt. His hair looked damp, as if he had just stepped out of the shower.

Kate straightened up defensively, his presence the catalyst for so many warring emotions within her that she felt the warm colour wash into her cheeks.

She swallowed hard. 'I'm sorry, I just had to pop in to see how she was. I know I shouldn't be here. . .'

'That makes two of us.' His mouth quirked. 'Do you suppose we'll get the sack?' He moved to plant a kiss on her nose before staring down at the baby. 'She looks better.'

'She is, thank goodness. She's taking fluids.'

He glanced up at her and said quietly, 'I suppose you do realise it's thanks to you?'

'Oh, come on, Sam. Let's not go through all that again. Surely the important thing is that she's going to make it?' She watched, fascinated, as his strong hand brushed with amazing gentleness against the baby's cheek.

'I wouldn't have given much for her chances a week ago.'

'Babies are amazingly resilient creatures,' she said briskly. She glanced up and wished she hadn't as her gaze was drawn to the sensuous mouth, the dark eyes, and she felt the pulse hammering in her throat as she raised her head to meet his gaze. 'You care, don't you?' she said through the sudden tightness in her throat.

'Of course I care.' His face darkened. 'Men aren't immune, you know? Women don't have a monopoly on emotion. Maybe men just get better at hiding their feelings.'

'It's nothing to be ashamed of, Sam. You're not invincible,' she snapped. 'None of us are. When we choose to be doctors we go into it knowing there are going to be good days as well as bad. No one said it would be easy, or that we'd get it right every time. We do the best we can and if, sometimes, it's not enough. . .'

She broke off as Sam's hands came down suddenly on her shoulders. Before she knew what was happening, he tilted her face up then, with a low groan, his mouth came down on hers in a punishing kiss.

For several seconds shock held her rigid before she began to struggle against his more powerful male strength. This wasn't supposed to be happening. She was angry—in theory. In practice, his kiss was playing havoc with her emotions, soothing her resistance until she moaned softly.

'This isn't fair, Sam.'

'I know.' His lips released hers fractionally, as his gaze explored her features. 'But I can't resist you when you're angry,' he breathed against her hair. 'If you knew how much I've been wanting to do that.'

She closed her eyes, willing herself to breathe evenly as his lips shifted their assault from her mouth to her ear lobes to her throat and back to her mouth as he kissed her again—very slowly.

Her hand rested against his chest, feeling the strong thudding of his heartbeat, his body so tantalisingly close. She tried to move away, shaken by the sudden realisation that her feelings towards him had undergone a subtle change even though she couldn't quite define it.

'I don't think this is a good idea, Sam,' she said huskily. 'I shouldn't be here. What if someone came along?'

'I imagine they might be a little shocked.' His voice was uneven as he raised his head to look at her. 'I'm not sure I care.'

She drew a deep breath as his head descended again, his mouth taking possession of hers with an aggressive thoroughness, forcing her lips apart as his tongue relentlessly invaded the softness of her mouth.

She gasped at the sensations that coursed through her, like a fire out of control as her body betrayed her with its instant response. In all the times Jeremy had kissed her it had never been like this.

Moaning softly, she swayed towards him. For an instant she felt him tense, his breathing harsh as he set her free—leaving her senses reeling in heated confusion. As she started to protest, she became dizzyingly aware of the open door and then, in one fluid movement, Sam was shielding her from view, giving her time to restore her clothes to some sort of order.

Her mouth felt swollen; she knew her cheeks were flushed and she was grateful for Sam's control as he turned to speak to the girl standing in the doorway.

'Ah, Doctor.' Julie Lyongi frowned as she shuffled a pile of notes and a large envelope. 'I'm so glad I caught you. Those urgent test results you wanted are ready.' She handed them to Sam, smiling apologetically at Kate. 'Oh, Dr Stewart, I'm so sorry, I didn't realise you were here. I can always come back later.'

'No.' Kate cleared her throat. 'No, it's all right.' She straightened her shoulders, purposely avoiding the sardonic gleam in Sam's eyes. 'I think we've said all we had to say,' she rasped.

'For now, maybe.' He raised a mocking eyebrow and she felt the colour flare into her cheeks again. 'We may need to discuss it further at some later date,' he said softly.

Kate choked. Damn you, Sam! she thought as she made her way across to the clinic. You are definitely not making this easy.

It was almost a relief to be kept so busy in the days that followed that she had no time to think about anything other than the job in hand.

She dealt methodically with chest infections, swabbed and treated ulcers, diagnosed a nasty case of screw worm and stitched wounds.

As always, to her surprise and infinite relief, she was able to rely heavily upon the enthusiastic young orderly, Simon Mxoli, who had, over the months, picked up the basic rudiments of nursing care and who, at the same time, acted happily as interpreter.

Time passed without her even being aware of it. One day she had become so engrossed in her work that it came as a shock to see Greg standing in the doorway, reminding her that she hadn't eaten since breakfast.

With a horrified glance at her watch, she saw that it was well past midday and, with profuse apologies, sent Simon away but remained sitting at the well-scrubbed table herself.

She brushed a hand through her hair, gesturing towards the queue which didn't seem to have diminished one iota. 'Honestly, Greg, I'm really not hungry and I think I ought to press on. I don't seem to be making any headway. Have you any idea what sort of chaos I'll come back to if I disappear now?'

'I can imagine,' he drawled cheerfully, coming over to the table to study her with amusement. 'You have dust on your nose.' He brushed it off. 'Very becoming, but not quite your shade.'

Ignoring her protests, he pulled her to her feet and helped her out of her white coat. 'Come on. I know Sam can be a bit of a slave-driver but we all have to eat, not to mention keeping up our fluids. Oh, and by the way,' he grinned as he tugged a bundle of letters from his pocket, 'I thought you might like to have these.'

'Letters?' She stared at them. 'You mean *real* letters—from home? For me?'

'Absolutely.' He waved them tantalisingly just out of her reach. 'The postman has been. Well, actually, one of the relief trucks called in and dropped them off with some supplies but, yes, we've had a delivery of mail.' Relenting, he handed her two envelopes.

Gazing at them, Kate instantly recognised her father's handwriting. The second seemed vaguely familiar, though she couldn't quite place it.

'Coming for lunch now?'

'I'm with you.' Grinning and hugging the letters to her, she sped after him, even though the possibility of seeing Sam for some reason added to her reluctance.

As they crossed the compound heat rose in distorting waves from the dry earth, but at least gradually her ears were becoming attuned to the different sounds of a world which was still relatively new to her and which, she knew, was already beginning to captivate her.

She was surprised at the speed with which it had happened, and with the awareness came also a depressing thought as she wondered how she would ever settle to a dull routine again when all this was over. How would she face life without Sam?

Wandering into the staff dining quarters they found Sanje helping himself to sandwiches and Jill already seated, deeply engrossed in her own letters.

Grinning, Greg handed Kate a plate, determinedly thrusting cutlery into her hands. 'Eat.'

'Anyone for coffee while I'm doing the honours?' Sanje helped himself from the Thermos jug which had been left on a tray.

'Now that definitely sounds like the best offer I've had all day so far.' Jill drained her own cup before handing it over. 'Three sugars.'

'Have you no soul?' Smiling, he refilled her cup and passed it back.

'I need all the energy I can get.' She stretched, stifling a yawn. 'Sometimes I have this nightmare, where I'm working on the ward and suddenly my feet disappear and I realise I'm melting.'

'God, I could eat a horse.' Greg's brow furrowed as he lifted the lid on one of the serving dishes, stirring the contents warily with a spoon. 'On second thoughts, I prefer mine lightly poached.'

Jill laughed. 'Actually, it's very nice. Try it—it's lamb curry.'

'Yes, well, I'll take your word for it. I think I'll stick to sandwiches.'

Finally settling for salad and fruit juice, Kate carried her food on a tray to one of the smaller tables where she made a perfunctory attempt at eating before opening her letters.

The contents of her father's was predictable. Chatty
and reassuring, as she read it she found herself battling
against a sudden overwhelming feeling of homesickness
as the words leapt out of the page:

> It snowed heavily last night. Needless to say, I
> was called out to Willowdale farm. Luckily the snow
> plough had been out to clear the road... The flu
> epidemic is finally over... Sad news, old Josh
> Hetherington finally died, aged eighty-nine, but he
> had a good innings.

Smiling, she let the letter fall and reached for the
other envelope. She was surprised to discover that it
was from Beth Read, who wrote:

> Life goes on. There are still never enough hours
> in the day. I miss having you around so don't get too
> attached to Africa. Oh, yes, and I thought you might
> like to know that Jeremy left St Maud's a few
> weeks ago...

Kate waited for the familiar pang of depression to
hit her, and was surprised when it didn't. So he and
Anna must be married, then? Well, she was glad for
them both. Perhaps Anna was the kind of wife Jeremy
needed.

But it might have been you, the thought flashed into
her mind and was dismissed instantly as she realised,
with a slight sense of shock, that she had never been
in love with Jeremy.

In fact, looking back, she sometimes wondered how
it had lasted as long as it did. They had drifted into a
relationship. Jeremy had been good company. They'd
had a lot in common. She'd been studying hard, still
hoping to qualify. Jeremy had been a year ahead of her
and he was ambitious.

So why had he left St Maud's? He had been in line for a senior registrar's job, she thought, a frown briefly furrowing her brow. Maybe something better had come up. Well she wished him—and Anna—well.

She was taken unawares as a fleeting, but none the less disturbing, image of Sam's attractive features flashed completely unbidden into her mind, and she wondered again what it would be like to be married to such a man.

She shook herself. What was she doing, daydreaming about a man she still hardly knew? Sexual attraction was one thing, marriage was quite another and if there was one thing she had learned in the past few months it was that the two didn't necessarily go together!

With a sigh, she picked up her fork and began to eat. In fact, the food was surprisingly good and she was surprised to find herself suddenly even more hungry than she had imagined. When she finally sat back, pushing her plate away, it was disconcerting to see Greg watching her with a glint of amusement in his eyes.

'For someone who wasn't hungry, I'd say you did pretty well. By the way, some good news, folks,' he raised his voice. 'You'll be pleased to hear that little Ben went home today. He's doing fine.'

A loud cheer greeted his words.

'One down, who knows how many more to go?' Greg murmured quietly, smiling as Kate glanced up. 'Still, it's progress, I suppose.'

She was helping herself to coffee when Sam walked in just as the others were slowly beginning to drift away. A harassed expression marred his attractive features.

A small pulse began to hammer at her throat as he poured himself coffee and she proffered the sugar. As he took it their fingers met, invoking so vivid a memory of his kiss that she jerked away—spilling coffee into the saucer.

'Problems?' she asked huskily.

He frowned. 'It sounds like it. I've had a call from the Kendall place.'

'Kendall?'

'Ted Kendall is a senior warden on one of the game reserves. They've had a spot of bother in recent months with poachers. It seems Ted and his son, Pete, have been hurt.'

She was instantly concerned. 'Seriously?'

His mouth tightened. 'All I know is that Pete has a gunshot wound. It sounds as if he's lost a lot of blood. I won't know how bad it is until I take a look.' He stirred his coffee. 'I said I'd go out there. Will you come with me? It'll give you a chance to meet Ted and Margaret at the same time. They're a nice couple.'

'I'd love to.' A tiny frisson of pleasure ran through her. 'Just give me time to get myself organised.'

'I'll be ready to leave in about half an hour.'

Draining her coffee, she fled to her room and headed for the shower. Thirty minutes later, dressed in jeans and a baggy green T-shirt and having changed her shoes for more practical boots, she hurried across the compound to where Sam was checking the equipment on board the truck.

'Sorry I kept you waiting,' she managed breathlessly. 'I had to check that the ward was covered before I could get changed.'

'It's OK; I had to make sure all the gear was on board, anyway.' He held out a hand to help her climb into the passenger seat, his gaze lingering for a few seconds on the figure-hugging jeans.

The sky was blue with only a few wisps of cloud. She was glad she had brought a hat, even though her hair already felt damp under it. Taking it off, she wiped a film of sweat from her forehead.

'How far is the Kendall place?'

'About an hour from here and I'd better warn you, some of it is pretty rough going.'

Kate hung on as they set off, her gaze straying anxiously to the rifle Sam had placed carefully in the back of the truck.

'I hope you're not expecting to have to use that.' She managed to smile as she said it.

He concentrated on keeping the vehicle steady on the dust road. 'It's just a precaution. I prefer not to take any chances.'

'I thought the problem of poachers was pretty much under control these days?'

He gave a wry laugh. 'If the stakes are big enough you'll always find someone prepared to take risks. People like Ted Kendall have spent a lifetime trying to stamp it out, but what happens is that the poachers become more resourceful. Believe me, it's still big business and we're not just talking ivory—it's animal organs as well as bones.'

She turned her head to look at him. 'The Kendalls are friends of yours?'

Sam didn't answer immediately. He needed all his concentration to keep the truck on the road. 'They're a nice couple. Margaret had a slight heart attack about twelve months ago. She got over it pretty well and she's a sensible lady, but that doesn't stop Ted worrying.' He gestured to her left. 'Elephant.'

It was a small herd, cows and a large bull. They moved slowly, with cumbersome grace, playfully stirring up clouds of dust.

'They're heading for the waterhole.'

Kate watched, entranced. 'It's hard to believe that something so big can be so beautiful, but they are.' She swallowed hard. 'How could anyone want to kill them?'

Sam slowed the truck to give her a better view. 'That's only a small group. They must have become separated from the main herd.'

'You mean there are more?'

'Back there.'

Involuntarily she glanced over his shoulder and felt his arm brush against her neck. He smelled of cologne and her skin tingled as he turned his head, his sensuous mouth drifting close to her cheek. She drew a long, shaky breath, pretending to be absorbed as a great bull moved out into the open, uneasily scenting the wind.

'We're between him and the main herd, surely?'

Amusement threaded his voice. 'Scared, Kate?'

She swallowed hard. 'The only elephants I've ever seen were in a zoo and that was quite close enough, thank you very much.'

She turned her head to study his profile, letting her gaze wander over the tanned features, absorbing the line of his jaw. He must think she was babbling like a schoolgirl, but there was nothing even remotely school-girlish about her growing awareness for this man.

In desperation she looked away. 'This is different. Not that I imagine we're in any real danger.'

His voice hardened. 'There's always danger with any wild animal. Don't ever make the mistake of taking anything for granted out here. There's always something looking for an easy meal.'

'Thanks for the warning—I'll bear it in mind next time I feel like taking a stroll.'

He grinned. 'All the same, they're getting restless. I think we'll make a move.' He let in the clutch, moving off slowly, and Kate released her breath slowly. The wild animals weren't the only thing to be wary of out here. There were other, far more subtle dangers—of the two-legged variety!

She pressed a hand to her throat. Even the breeze, caused by the truck's movement, was hot and the dust thrown up from the wheels made conversation awkward.

She moistened her dry lips with her tongue. 'Does it ever rain around here?'

'In theory there are two rainy seasons. The short

one in spring and the heavier rains in November.'

She glanced at him. 'In theory?'

His face darkened. 'There aren't any guarantees.'

She stared out at the ripening maize. 'So what will happen if it doesn't rain? What about the crops?'

The truck hit a rut and he battled to bring it back under control. 'If it's just late they'll probably survive. If we don't get any rain at all. . .' he shrugged '. . .the harvest will fail.'

'But. . .that's awful.'

'It won't be the first time, Kate, and it certainly won't be the last. This is a country of extremes. When it does rain it's as if a miracle takes place.' He followed the direction of her gaze to the dry, cracked soil. 'Maybe it really is a miracle, but within the space of a few hours the lakes will fill and what you see out there will be transformed into a green carpet. There'll even be flowers.'

'In a few hours?'

His mouth twisted. 'We're not talking English April showers; we're talking more rain than you've probably ever seen. I've seen a dried-up river bed turn into a raging torrent.'

She fanned her cheeks with her hat. Sam reached into the back of the truck, handing her a Thermos of juice. She drank gratefully, relishing the liquid despite its warmth.

Sam nodded at the distance behind them. 'See those hills?'

She turned her head, staring across the hazy, heat-distorted miles, overawed by the unreality of it all. She unbuttoned her shirt a little further as the air grew steadily hotter.

'From the top you can see across a hundred miles of the Rift Valley.'

She could believe it. Out here anything seemed possible.

Sam drove steadily, his hands tanned and relaxed against the steering-wheel. Patches of sweat darkened his shirt, but he seemed untroubled by the heat.

It seemed hard to imagine that she might ever become accustomed to it too, yet in spite of it she felt the excitement building up in her as she caught a glimpse of a herd of zebra, grazing undisturbed.

She had to keep telling herself that it wasn't all part of a dream. It was easy to see why people fell in love with this country. How would she ever go back to St Maud's? she wondered. How could her life ever be the same again?

Her eyes ranged the countryside and, without even being aware of it, she sighed.

'Tired?'

'What? Oh, no.' Smiling, she gave herself a mental shake. 'More shell-shocked, I think. There's so much to take in.'

'I know what you mean.' He took his eyes briefly from the road to glance at her. 'It takes a bit of getting used to.'

She frowned. 'It's funny, but I had a picture in my mind of what Africa would be like. I'd seen pictures; read books but. . .' she shook her head '. . .nothing really prepares you for all of this. It's breathtaking. There are so many contrasts. It's so. . .so vast.' Her smile flickered up at him. 'Don't you ever get lonely, so far from home?'

Instantly, as she sensed the tautening of his muscles, she wished the words unsaid. 'I. . .I'm sorry, that was tactless of me. I shouldn't have said it, especially as. . .' She broke off, appalled by the realisation that she was getting in deeper still.

'You were saying?' Sam prompted softly.

She felt the colour flare into her cheeks. 'I'm sorry. I heard about your divorce.' She bit at her lower lip. 'We weren't gossiping. Greg just mentioned it in passing. I think he assumed I knew. . .'

'Forget it; it's not a problem,' Sam advised in a hard voice. 'I know what small communities are like—villages, hospitals, whatever. If your wife walks out the whole world knows about it.'

'I'm sorry,' she said again, moistening her dry lips with her tongue. 'You must have been devastated.'

He shrugged. 'It probably sounds crazy, but I'm not sure what I felt. In any case, there are two sides to every coin. Maybe I should have been more aware of what was happening but I was very involved in what I was doing. I wasn't just fund-raising, I was working out my contract at the hospital and preparing for my trip to Ramindi.' His mouth tightened. 'At that stage it was planned that I'd be here for six months.'

He gave a slight laugh but there was no mirth in the sound. 'All in all, it didn't leave much time for social life.'

Kate gave him a long, searching look. 'But surely your wife understood? I mean. . .'

For a second there was a flash of cynicism in his eyes. 'Sara wasn't in the medical profession. She worked for the local radio station. It's ironic, really. That was how we met. She did a piece on our fund-raising project. God knows, we were glad of the publicity. Sara and I got to know each other and it went on from there.'

'But surely she realised when she agreed to marry you that that's what being a doctor is all about? We know before we enter medical school that it's not going to be a nine to five job.'

'It's never that simple,' Sam sighed. 'I'd had time to think about it. I knew what I was letting myself in for. There was no reason why Sara should share my enthusiasm for Ramindi. I knew it was up and running, with George in charge, but it needed funds to keep it going. You know how things are out here.'

Kate felt her anger stirring. 'But why do you blame yourself? Surely she must have known what it meant to you?'

A spasm flickered across his face. 'Perhaps we were both naïve. We were young. It was all exciting. Sara liked people; she loved her job. We thought it could work. In any case—' his mouth twisted '—don't they say absence makes the heart grow fonder? Well, in our case it didn't work. Maybe it wasn't fair of me to expect her to wait.'

'What happened?'

'I managed to get a few days' unexpected leave. I got a lift back to Nairobi in the supply plane and caught the first flight home, expecting to surprise her.'

His dark brows drew together. 'She wasn't there. At first I didn't think anything of it. I waited—and waited. Finally I realised she wasn't going to come home. I thought maybe she'd gone to stay with a friend so I rang around.' He gave a wry smile. 'I was right. The only problem was—it was a male friend and it wasn't the first time.'

Kate felt her anger stirring. 'What did you do?'

He shrugged. 'She came home, eventually, in the early hours of the morning. We talked—heatedly. Sara said she'd met someone else. She packed a bag and left. I came back to Africa, by which time George was struggling to cope, anyway. So I extended my contract and stayed.'

'Do. . .do you have any idea where she is now?'

She felt her heart give an erratic thud as he turned his head to look at her. 'The last I heard she had married a television producer. She's moved up in the world; something of a household name these days—reading the news.'

Kate stared at him. 'Not. . . You don't mean. . .?'

'The very same.'

'Oh, Sam, I'm so sorry.'

His mouth tightened. 'Don't be. If I learned anything it was not to make the same mistake twice. At least there weren't any children.'

'Did you want them?' she said softly.

'They weren't an option. I don't think about it.'

Kate shivered in spite of the heat as she became aware, yet again, of the depths of emotion Sam was capable of. There was a core of vulnerability about him, rarely seen, never touched. It would be so easy to fall in love with this man, but would he ever again want to take a chance on love?

She saw him frown and heard his soft intake of breath as he took one hand from the wheel to brush it gently against her cheek, setting her heart thudding from the brief contact.

She found herself gazing in rapt fascination as, for a second, his face loomed closer, bringing with it the utterly sensuous mouth.

Her own hand rose to cover his. She closed her eyes, breathing deeply as another new sensation came homing in on her bemused senses. It was already too late. She was in love with Sam Brady and there was absolutely no future in it. He had made it perfectly clear that he wasn't about to repeat the mistakes of the past. The trouble was that, feeling as she did, fighting him might be a whole lot easier than fighting her own emotions.

In desperation she drew away. 'Keep your eyes on the road, Sam,' she said, breathlessly.

She heard the quiet rumble of laughter in his throat. 'Coward,' he said softly.

She didn't look at him. He was right; she *was* scared—scared stiff that she was already way out of her depth where he was concerned.

CHAPTER EIGHT

IT WAS almost a relief when they reached the Kendall place at last.

Sam cut the engine and was reaching for his bag as Margaret Kendall came down the steps to greet them, her face anxious.

In her sixties, she was still an attractive woman. Born in South Africa, she was tall, her greying blonde hair was swept back, secured by a scarf, and she wore a short-sleeved cotton dress.

'Sam, it's good of you to get here so quickly. I can't tell you how worried I've been.'

'How's Ted?'

'Frustrated.' She gave a slight laugh. 'You know how he is—hates not being able to do what he wants to do.' Her tanned face was wreathed in lines of concern. 'He says he's all right but he took a pretty hard knock on the head. I'm more worried about Pete. He's lost a lot of blood, Sam. I've done the best I can to make him comfortable.'

'I'll take a look at him.' Sam squeezed her shoulder. 'And Ted's right—you're not to worry. He's a tough old nut and Pete takes after him.' He unloaded the emergency kit and they headed for the bungalow. 'By the way, this is Dr Stewart—Kate Stewart. I thought it would be a chance for the two of you to meet.'

'Dr Stewart.' Margaret Kendall held out her hand. 'It's always good to see a new face. I just wish it could have been under better circumstances.'

Kate smiled. 'Please, call me Kate. I'm sure Sam will soon get things sorted out.'

'You'd better come inside.' Margaret led them,

without preamble, into the cooler interior of the wooden-built bungalow.

Sam glanced briefly at the man seated in the chair. 'What's this, then, Ted? In the wars again?' He put the emergency kit down. 'What happened—can you remember?'

'Course I can remember.' Ted Kendall swore softly. 'We'd had a warning there might be trouble. Someone spotted a gang of poachers on our patch a few days ago, then we found a butchered bull elephant. It was still pretty fresh so we knew they couldn't be too far ahead of us.' He shook his head and winced. 'They were closer than we realised. Took us by surprise.'

'Let's take a look.' Sam gently eased aside the blood-stained cloth the man was holding to a wound at the back of his head. 'Hmm, you're going to have a nasty bump there.' He peered closer. 'Margaret's done a pretty good job of cleaning it up but you might need a couple of stitches.'

'I'll be fine.' Ted waved them away. 'Just see to young Pete. He's not looking too good.'

Sam had already moved to crouch beside the younger man. His eyes were closed, his skin was pale and blood stained the front and left sleeve of his shirt.

'Pete, it's Sam here—Sam Brady. I just want to take a look; see what the damage is.'

Pete Kendall's eyelids fluttered open briefly. 'Good to see you, Doc.'

'Just lie still; let me do all the work.'

'Tell you the truth, I wasn't thinking of going any-where right now.' He managed a laugh before moaning slightly and closing his eyes again.

Sam's mouth twitched. 'I'm glad to hear it. I'll try not to hurt you but I may have to dig around a bit. If the bullet is still in there I need to know where it's lying.'

Kate had already opened the medical kit, laying it

out on a small table, before her fingers went automatically to the man's wrist, feeling for a pulse as she made her own rapid, visual assessment of his condition.

His breathing was shallow and his skin felt clammy. For the first time the realisation hit her that they might have to operate. She watched as Sam eased aside the torn shirt, peering closely at the wound. 'How bad is it?'

'It's a bit of a mess.' Sam spoke calmly beside her. 'Have you ever seen a gunshot wound before?'

She gave a slight smile. 'We didn't come across too many poachers in Foxleigh, I'm pleased to say.'

His hand tightened briefly, warm and reassuring, on her shoulder. 'This one's a bit nasty,' he said quietly. 'The bullet is still in there. I was hoping it might have passed straight through, but no such luck.' He looked at her. 'Have you ever done any surgery?'

'No.' She swallowed hard. 'I've watched but. . . I'll cope. You'll just have to tell me what you want me to do.'

'Good girl.'

With an effort she summoned a smile, feeling the colour mounting in her cheeks. Sam crouched beside Pete Kendall again.

'Pete, we're going to have to get the bullet out.'

Margaret Kendall pressed a hand to her mouth, glancing around the room. 'But can you. . .? I mean, here?'

'We don't have any choice.' Sam straightened up, lowering his voice slightly. 'The bullet has to come out, and soon, before any infection sets in.' He glanced at her pale features. 'Are you OK?'

'Sure.' The older woman swallowed hard. 'Just tell me what you need.'

'We'll have to use the kitchen. We'll need to get the place scrubbed up.'

'I'll help.' Margaret was already heading for the door, until Sam's voice drew her to a halt.

'Better show us where everything is, then leave it to

us, Maggie. Besides,' he smiled, 'I think Ted could do with a little moral support right now.'

Kate guessed that his response had deliberately been calculated to put the older woman at ease. Margaret Kendall seemed to hesitate and then nodded, reaching for her husband's hand. 'Right, you carry on.'

'He's going to be all right, Maggie. It'll be over before you know it.' He watched her hurry away, a look of intense relief on her face, before he turned to his patient. 'We're going to get the bullet out and make you feel more comfortable, Pete. Just try to relax; leave everything to us.'

The semi-conscious man weakly raised a hand in a gesture of acquiescence and let it fall. Sam looked at Kate and said softly, 'I'd better give him a quick medical check-up.' He uncoiled his stethoscope and Kate nodded.

'I'll set up the equipment.'

Ten minutes later, having unpacked the emergency equipment, she turned to Sam and realised with a sense of shock that he had stripped off his shirt and was waiting for her to tie the tapes on his operating gown.

With fingers that fumbled she did so, then met his gaze above the operating mask.

'Hopefully it's going to be a simple, straightforward procedure. He's lost a lot of blood but the wound looks pretty clean.'

She looked at him, anxiety clouding her eyes. 'Surgery isn't my field, Sam. What if I let you down?'

'You won't,' he said, with a confidence she wished she shared. 'Just watch what I do and you'll be fine.' Above the mask his eyes smiled. 'Scout's honour.'

She nodded, knowing that her own attempt at a smile didn't reach her eyes. Almost defensively she turned away, swallowing hard on the knot of emotion that suddenly tightened her throat. It wasn't the job she was worried about—her nervousness had more to do with the man himself, and the growing awareness of the disturbing effect his nearness seemed to be having on her nerves.

It was a relief to be able to busy herself with checking the instruments, deliberately giving herself time to bring her thoughts back under control.

In the months since Jeremy's betrayal she had slowly begun to build up a protective barrier around her shattered emotions. She thought she had succeeded—until now. She closed her eyes, afraid that Sam might see what was happening to her.

Coming to Africa was supposed to be part of the healing process—the fresh start she had felt she so desperately needed. It was only now that she realised that her feelings for Jeremy bore no relation to what she was experiencing now, with this man.

'OK?'

'What?' She blinked hard, staring up to see him frowning over his mask. 'Oh, yes, fine. I'm just a little nervous, that's all.'

'There's nothing to worry about, I promise.' He gave an encouraging grin. 'Take a few deep breaths. You'll be fine.'

If only it was that simple, the thought hung over her. She nodded, her fingers trembling as she made a final check of the instruments carefully laid out in front of her. She had to stop thinking like this, she told herself. Stop thinking about everything except the job in hand. Taking a deep breath, she took refuge behind a screen of professionalism.

Sam worked in silence, apart from an occasional, softly worded request. 'Swab here. Bring the light closer.' A nod as she complied, anticipating his needs.

It was a fascinating experience to watch Sam work, Kate thought. Almost without being aware of it, they became a team, any initial nervousness on her part slipping away as her actions became automatic and her medical training took over.

Throughout, Sam's voice was calm, decisive, authoritative. There was no time for emotion as the blood was swabbed away and she concentrated on what was happening as, with a deft economy of movement, Sam cleaned and inspected the wound.

'He's damn lucky.' His voice was slightly muffled by the mask. 'The bullet missed any vital organs. That was my main worry.'

Kate lost all track of time, conscious only of the taut line of Sam's body and her own tension. She passed the back of her arm over her forehead, wiping away a thin film of sweat.

Once she fumbled for an instrument and could only watch in horror as it clattered noisily to the floor. She stared at it, appalled by her own clumsiness.

'Forget it. Just hand me another,' came the quiet response.

She did so, breathing deeply behind her mask and forcing herself to concentrate. Moments later, with a grunt of satisfaction, Sam dropped the offending bullet into a steel dish.

'Nasty-looking little item.' Flexing his hands, he bent over the unconscious man once more. 'This is the easy part. We close him up, clean him up and call it a day.' Amazingly, Kate found herself treated to a smile as Sam glanced briefly in her direction. 'Hang on in there. We're almost done.'

Minutes later he straightened up, tugging his mask down. 'OK, that's it; you can relax.' His hand rested briefly on her shoulder and she felt the colour surge into her cheeks. 'Let's just get cleaned up and give the Kendalls the good news, shall we? They must be worried sick.'

Half an hour later, her relief all too evident, Margaret Kendall handed them glasses of ice-cold beer. 'We'll never be able to thank you enough.' Returning to her seat, she held her husband's hand. 'It was a shock, seeing Pete like that. The thought of. . .that we might lose him. . .' She broke off.

Ted Kendall cleared his throat awkwardly. 'Our youngest boy, Neil, was killed four years ago in a riding accident,' he explained quietly, patting his wife's hand. 'Some days you think you're over it but then it comes back to hit you, especially when something like this happens.' He spoke calmly but behind the faint smile Kate couldn't help but catch a faint note of desperation.

She swallowed hard. 'I'm so sorry. I had no idea.'

'Pete's going to be fine,' Sam put in quietly, pressing a hand to the older man's shoulder. 'The bullet made a clean entry. I know it looked messy but, by some miracle, it missed all the vital organs. He's lost a lot of blood and he's probably going to feel as if he's been kicked by a bull for the next few days, but he's going to make a complete recovery, provided he behaves sensibly.'

'Don't you worry on that score,' Margaret said. 'I won't let him out of my sight.' She flicked a glance at her husband. 'They'll both be doing as they're told from now on.'

'I'll leave some antibiotics, just to be on the safe side, and some painkillers.' Sam handed her a couple of bottles. 'If you're worried at all give me a call.'

'Don't you worry, I'll make sure they take them.' Margaret followed them to the door and out onto the veranda, shading her eyes against the sun. She smiled at Kate. 'We don't get to see too many faces around here. Pity we won't be around long enough to get better acquainted.'

'You're not leaving?'

Margaret Kendall looked at Sam and smiled wryly. 'We made the decision at last. Well, it makes sense. Ted's retiring in a couple of months. I've finally managed to persuade him that he's too old for this sort of thing.' She gave a slight laugh. 'After what's happened today I don't reckon I'll get any more arguments.'

'Where will you go?'

Margaret looked at Kate. 'Ted doesn't know it yet but we're going to England for a holiday to visit the family. He's got brothers he hasn't seen in twenty years. I've got a sister. They've all got kids. At our age you can't afford to waste time. Life's precious—I'm even more sure of that now. You have to take your chances when you can. So we're having a bit of a farewell do—just a small party.'

She lowered her voice conspiratorially and said, with more than a hint of pride in her voice, 'We have a pretty special anniversary coming up too. Forty-five years.' Her smile faded slightly.

'I reckon it's time we did some of the things we've always wanted to do. Ted loves his job and I'm not saying we haven't had a good life, but none of us is getting any younger. I reckon it's time we let the younger ones take over.' The smile was in evidence again. 'So, we're having a bit of a do, as I said. I shall give Ted the air tickets and have him on that plane so fast his feet won't touch the floor.'

Sam grinned as he kissed her on the cheek. 'Good luck to you, Maggie. I hope it all works out for you. Just take things easy.'

Minutes later, their goodbyes said, they were loading their gear back onto the truck. The early evening sun was slightly cooler and a breeze helped to freshen the air.

Kate hoisted the last of the bags into the truck and lifted the heavy swathe of her hair from her neck, realising that she was suddenly very tired.

Closing her eyes briefly, she pushed a strand of hair from her eyes. The thought of stripping off her clothes and standing under a cold shower rose tantalisingly in her mind, only to be pushed away as she opened her eyes and became aware of Sam watching her.

With a sudden movement she turned away and swayed slightly, pressing a hand to her eyes.

In an instant Sam was there. Involuntarily she reached out, blushing as she realised that her fingers were clamped firmly on to his arm. Swallowing hard, she relinquished her grip.

'Are you all right?'

'I'm fine.' She licked her dry lips and, with an effort, managed a slight laugh. 'Actually, I'm still shaking.' She held out her hands, seeing them tremble. 'Thank God you were here. I could never have done what you did.'

'It's nothing to be ashamed of, Kate. You did well. I couldn't have managed without you.'

'I've never seen a gunshot wound before. I've read about this sort of thing. I know poaching still goes on but. . .' She raised her head to look at him. 'Sam, I had no idea the Kendalls had already lost a son. It's hard to imagine the sort of torment they must have been going through, thinking it could be about to happen all over again. I don't think I'd have that sort of courage.'

'Ted loves his job. It's what he knows—open spaces, animals. . .'

'Danger, Sam. We're talking danger.'

His dark brows drew together. 'Things are changing, slowly. A few years ago the elephant was in danger of being wiped out as a species. Ivory made big money. It's thanks to Ted and people like him that the herds are increasing again. He knows the risks involved and so does Pete.'

'He'll stay on when his father leaves?'

'Of course. Why not? If you'd grown up out here would you willingly want to leave all this?'

She had to admit that there was a magic about Africa. Already it had begun to weave a spell and she wondered, with a sudden sense of desolation, how she was going to feel when it was her turn to say goodbye. In more ways than one, she knew her life could never be the same again.

Shading her eyes, she gazed into the hazy distance. 'It is beautiful,' she breathed. 'Far more beautiful than I'd ever imagined.' She darted a look at Sam's profile, only to find him studying her in a way she found oddly disturbing. She drew a deep breath and deliberately made a play of reaching for the last of the boxes. 'I can understand why the Kendalls would be loath to leave. Forty-five years is a long time.'

'Yes, it is. They're nice people. Here, you'd better let me.'

'No, it's fine. I can manage.' But he had taken the boxes from her and had somehow, in the process, drawn her towards him. 'They're obviously happy,' she said faintly, her eyes widening with confusion as, very slowly, he tilted her chin to trace the curve of her mouth with his thumb.

'They're crazy about each other,' he murmured softly. His gaze narrowed. She felt him tense and heard his soft intake of breath, then he was tilting her face up and kissing her—very slowly and with a thoroughness that left her head reeling.

'If you knew how much I've been wanting to do this.' His voice was uneven as he ran his hands through her hair. He frowned as she looked at him, her grey eyes clouded with uncertainty. 'Kate. . .'

She told herself it was crazy; that she could put a stop to this now. What she hadn't counted on was the spontaneous response of every nerve in her body that simply being close to this man seemed to evoke.

Her hand rested against his chest, the strong, lean body so tantalisingly close, then she gasped as she felt a surge of pure physical awareness as the sensuous mouth ground against hers. Desire licked like a flame as she began to lose control beneath the touch of his hands.

'I'm not sure this is a good idea, Sam,' she breathed. She felt dazed by her reactions to the tumult of sensations it seemed he could always arouse whenever she was in his arms. Pleasure, confusion, everything happening too fast, moving beyond her control. 'Don't you think we should be getting back?'

'There's plenty of time.' His voice sounded rough-edged. 'I'm not even sure I want to go back.'

She sensed him tensing and found herself watching in rapt fascination as his mouth descended again. She knew she should call a halt now. 'Please, Sam, don't. . .' she protested weakly.

He drew a ragged breath as he looked at her for a long moment as he pulled her roughly towards him. 'My God, I wonder if you have any idea of the effect you have on me?'

She moaned softly as his mouth came down on hers, making teasing advances against her cheek, to the hollow of her throat and back to her mouth—claiming it with a fierce possession that left them both breathless.

'Sam, this is crazy. . .'

'Tell me you want me as much as I want you, Kate,' he ground out.

'Sam, this isn't fair.' Her body quivered beneath the onslaught. She moaned as his hands slid beneath her shirt, discovering the exquisite fullness of her breasts. She was rapidly losing control beneath the feather-light touch of his fingers.

She stood very still—eyes closed, breathing deeply—afraid he might see what was happening to her. In desperation she tried to break away but his grasp merely tightened on her shoulders, sending warning signals to her brain.

'Don't fight it, Kate,' he said, huskily. 'There's nothing to be afraid of. You must know I'd never do anything to hurt you.'

Not knowingly, maybe, she thought. But she was already out of her depth, fighting for her life.

'I want you, Kate,' he rasped. 'I want to make love to you. Have you any idea how much I need you?'

He tried to draw her back into the circle of his arms. Her throat tightened. *Need, want.* But there was a world of difference between wanting and loving. Love needed a two-sided commitment and that was the one thing that Sam wasn't prepared to give.

She closed her eyes in a feeble and totally unsuccessful attempt to shut him out of her thoughts. She might have known that it wouldn't work. How could it when he only had to be near her for the wild impulses to start racing up and down her spine? It was so unfair.

'Please, no,' she protested weakly and heard him groan softly. She stiffened in his arms, saw the turmoil in his eyes and panicked as she sensed how little it would take to make her surrender completely to this man if he kissed her again.

Her hands pushed against his chest. 'Don't do this to me, Sam.'

'Do what?' he murmured, huskily.

'Don't make me want you,' she whispered. 'I can't think.'

'Then don't.' His mouth sought and found hers, forcing a sweet invasion and teasing her lips into a quivering response with the slow, sensuous glide of his tongue.

A tremor ran through her. She pulled away, her soft mouth trembling and her eyes dilated in her flushed face. 'Don't you see, Sam, none of this is real.'

'Not real!' He gave a harsh laugh. 'It's as real as anything gets. I know you've been hurt,' he rasped, 'but we have to move on, Kate. Sometimes we have to take risks.'

She couldn't argue with that—with any of it. But wasn't he asking her to take the biggest risk of all? A relationship without the ultimate commitment?

His hands were on her shoulders. 'I could persuade you, Kate.'

'I know.' A tremor ran through her. 'That's what I'm afraid of.' She was aware of his taut face, frowning down at her. 'I. . .I'm sorry.' She brushed the back of her hand against her mouth, blushing as she realised that the buttons of her blouse were unfastened. She drew them quickly together.

'Don't be,' he rasped. 'I'm the one who should be sorry.' A nerve pulsed in his jaw and then, abruptly, he released her. 'You're right—we should be getting back.'

They drove back to the hospital in virtual silence—like strangers, Kate thought, turning her head to stare unseeingly out of the window.

This was ridiculous. She blinked hard on the tears that suddenly welled up to sting at her eyes. Common sense told her that it was best this way, ended now before anyone got hurt. Some things were best avoided and Sam Brady definitely came into that category. But, ridiculous or not, it didn't explain why she should feel so cheated.

CHAPTER NINE

In SPITE of feeling exhausted Kate slept badly that night, tossing and turning as her mind refused to switch off from the day's events.

Several times, glancing at the clock, she sighed and reshaped her pillows, determinedly closing her eyes. She needed her sleep, she told herself irritably. The last thing she should be doing was lying here trying to erase the memory of a very disturbing kiss from her mind.

It must have been almost dawn before her eyes finally closed and she fell into a deep sleep, only to be woken—seconds later, it seemed—by the sound of the alarm and the sun shining warmly onto her face.

Groaning, Kate opened one eye to glare accusingly at the clock before reaching for her robe and heading for the shower.

Fifteen minutes later, having swallowed a cup of strong, black coffee, she made her way to the hospital. The sun was already hot and getting hotter. Glancing up at the sky, she saw that the few wisps of cloud had, over the past few days, gradually become a gathering blanket of heat and it came as something of a shock to realise that, almost without her noticing it, October had slid into November and that Christmas was only a few weeks away!

Jill was tepid-sponging a baby as Kate moved to join her. Her face wore a look of concern as she straightened up, drying her hands before looking up to smile a brief acknowledgement of Kate's arrival.

'Hi, I wonder if you'd take a look at this little chap before you do your round? He came in about an hour ago. I'm a bit worried about him.'

Kate looked at the infant lying in the metal-framed cot and felt the breath catch in her throat. His eyes were closed, he was seriously underweight and he was coughing—a harsh, hacking sound. He couldn't be more than about nine months old, she realised with a sense of shock.

As she looked more closely, she could see a fading rash across the tiny forehead and around the area of his ears and chest. His nose was running and his eyes were watering.

'Hmm, he's not looking too good, is he? Poor little mite. What's his temperature?'

'Thirty-eight point nine when I checked about ten minutes ago. That's why I thought I'd try the tepid sponging to see if I could bring it down a little.'

Kate nodded. 'You did the right thing. Any idea when the symptoms started? Have you spoken to the mum?'

'The parents are Masai. They thought the baby had a cold but then the fever started and he seemed to be going rapidly downhill from there.'

Taking her stethoscope from her pocket, Kate leaned forward to listen to the tiny chest. It was ridiculous but somehow she had never quite overcome a resistance to working with children, and more especially tiny babies. Their vulnerability punched a gaping hole in the cloak of professionalism she had always otherwise been able to build around her.

There was something about seeing a child in pain that knocked back every one of her carefully built defences.

Even in medical school it had inhibited her to the point where she had begun to have serious doubts about her ability to complete her studies simply because, unlike the majority of her senior colleagues, she had never quite managed to acquire the kind of detachment that was so necessary sometimes to become a doctor.

She felt those doubts bubbling up again now as she listened to the rattling sounds inside the tiny chest.

Straightening, she sighed. 'It doesn't sound too good in there. I'd say he's got a chest infection. Any signs of diarrhoea?'

'Afraid so.'

Kate pulled a face. 'I hate to disturb him too much, but I need to check his eyes and ears.' She reached for her ophthalmoscope. The baby jerked suddenly and began to whimper feebly, his tiny limbs flailing. She blinked hard, biting at her lip and starting suddenly as she became aware of the figure moving quietly to stand beside her.

Sam's coat brushed against her arm as he peered over her shoulder. 'I came over to pick up some reports.' He leaned forward and the faint smell of aftershave assailed her nostrils. 'Not looking too happy, is he? What do you think? Measles?'

'It's looking very much like it.'

It was amazing, really, Kate thought, watching fascinatedly as he gently stroked a finger against the baby's cheek until the whimpering gradually ceased. She obviously wasn't the only one to be affected by him! She drew a sharp breath.

'Are you all right?' Sam asked casually.

'I'm fine.' Her wandering thoughts brought the colour to her cheeks. 'It must be the heat...or something.'

'It happens.' A faint glimmer of humour lit his eyes, then he took the ophthalmoscope from her nerveless fingers. 'I'll bet you've got a pretty nasty headache, haven't you, little fellow? Let's just take a look at your eyes, shall we?' He shone the light into the baby's eyes, frowning at the yellow discharge crusted on the dark lashes. 'Hmm, not very nice, is it?' he murmured soothingly. 'Well, he's certainly got conjunctivitis,' he announced, seconds later. 'You've listened to his chest?'

Kate nodded. 'It's infected.'

'Not got a lot going for him, has he, poor little chap? Checked his mouth?'

'I was just about to. . .'

'Fascinating things, Koplik's spots. Look, there they are—the little devils.' Sam gently eased open the baby's mouth and Kate could clearly see the distinctive white spots. 'The danger in malnourished infants is cancrum oris, a gangrenous infection.'

She swallowed hard on the dryness of her throat. 'I'll get him started on penicillin straight away.'

'You'll find the cough will probably respond to pro-methazine, and you could try antibiotic drops for the conjunctivitis. We've found it works.' Sam looked at his watch as Kate followed him to the door. 'You'll probably find the family will want to stay with him.'

'Yes, we're making arrangements.' She looked at him and brushed a hand through her hair. 'It's crazy, I know, but I still can't get used to the idea that out here children can still die of a disease we think of back home as a minor childhood ailment.'

His mouth tightened fractionally. 'There's a difference. These kids have no natural resistance. They're undernourished. Most of their traditional grazing lands are gone. These days the Masai live on a diet of maize, beans and potatoes. They call it Kikuyan food. It isn't their natural diet—it's what they've had to become accustomed to.'

Kate moistened her dry lips with her tongue. 'I had no idea.'

His mouth twisted. 'There's no reason why you should. You can't learn everything in a few weeks. It's the way things are out here. I've been here longer than you. I can still be shocked by the things I see. There's no shame in it.'

She was appalled to find her eyes filling with tears. 'Look, I'm grateful for what you did. I didn't handle it very well. I don't. . .'

He looked at her for a few seconds before he cupped her face in his hand, forcing her to look at him. 'Don't ever be afraid of your emotions, Kate,' he said softly. 'We're doctors but that doesn't mean we can work magic. There'll never be any easy answers.'

She sniffed hard and gave a slight smile. 'Thanks, you always say the nicest things.'

'I do my best, ma'am,' he drawled softly as his lean fingers fastened gently on her shoulders, drawing her towards him to kiss her fleetingly on her mouth. Her lips parted hesitantly beneath his. He sighed and released her, glancing at his watch. 'I shouldn't be here. I'm supposed to be on the wards. By the way, who's on the clinic run this afternoon?'

'I am.'

'In that case, I'll see you later.' Smiling, he raised a hand. 'Call me if you need me.'

Like right now? The thought was pushed away as quickly as it arose. Tears burned at the back of her eyelids. She blinked them away. She loved Sam but how could she admit it to this man who, while he wanted her, made no secret of the fact that that was as far as his commitment went. She would have to accept him on those terms and she wasn't sure she could do that— not if it meant knowing that he would never return her love.

It needed an effort of will to return to the ward; to force her mind back to what she should be doing.

The baby's parents were standing beside the cot as she made her way along the ward. The mother, whose name was Mumai, was weeping softly. She was beautiful—dark-skinned and wearing the colourful, decorative beadwork which Kate recognised as being worn by both men and women among the Masai. Kate guessed that the girl was probably about eighteen years old. She was wailing softly.

'*Toto. Yeiyo.*'

'What is she saying?' she asked Jill.

'Child, her child. *Yeiyo* means mother. He's her first-born.'

'*Kaiyai. Enkai naishoo enkarra enkerai.*'

Jill blinked hard, turning away on the pretext of tidying away the equipment. 'She calls him the one sent by God. She calls him the child from God that gave me name.'

With an effort, Kate managed to force a smile. 'Tell her we are going to do everything we can to make her baby better. In the meantime, they are welcome to stay—to be with him. I'll write him up for the medication. The sooner we get it started the better. Keep up the fluids.' She wrote up the notes. 'I'll pop back later and take another look at him.'

'Will do.'

'Right, now I'd better take a quick look at the rest. . .'

'I don't think you'll find too many problems there,' Jill grinned. 'It's getting decidedly noisy, a sure sign that most of them are nearly ready to go home.'

'In that case I might even get through the clinic list before lunch.'

Optimism that was not confirmed as she crossed the parched grass where the inevitable queue had already begun to form.

'Good morning, Doctor.' Tomanke Waithaka, one of the orderlies, greeted her arrival with a grin. 'Maybe today it will rain.'

Glancing at the sky, Kate gave a short laugh. 'It's a nice thought, Tomanke, but I won't hold my breath.' She guessed that within an hour the heat would be close to unbearable.

'Good morning, Dr Stewart.' Julie Lyongi, looking— as always—frustratingly cool in her short-sleeved white dress, made a final check of the dressings trolley before looking up to smile at Kate.

'It looks as if we're in for a busy morning. Give me

a couple of minutes to get myself organised, then bring in the first patient.' Shrugging herself into a clean white coat and gathering up the cards, Kate made her way to her room, where shutters on the windows at least helped to keep out some of the heat.

She was right about it being a busy morning. Completing her examination of her latest patient, she checked the blood pressure of the man lying on the examination couch, noting at the same time the clammy coldness of his skin and his sunken eyes.

Daniel Warungu was fifty years old and had been suffering severe diarrhoea for the past five days.

Careful to avoid any change of expression so as not to alarm the man, Kate spoke softly to Julie. 'His blood pressure is very low and he's obviously seriously dehydrated. Has he been vomiting?'

'Yes, he says it began suddenly.'

'What about pain?' She waited as Julie spoke to the man.

'He says he is getting bad muscular cramps.'

'That will be due to the dehydration.' Kate made a very gentle examination of the man's abdomen. She frowned. 'I gather he has no control over the diarrhoea. It just flushes out.'

Julie nodded. 'That's right.'

'Has he described what happens afterwards?'

In response to gentle questioning, the man briefly opened his eyes and lifted one blue-veined hand as he spoke.

'It's all right,' Kate murmured soothingly. 'What did he say?'

'That there is more—like water, but not water.'

'Like rice water,' Kate nodded, frowning. 'He's in a bad way. I'm pretty sure this is cholera. We'll need a rectal swab to identify the organism.' She wrote up the notes as she was speaking.

'I'll see to it straight away.'

'We need to be absolutely certain this isn't food poisoning or viral enteritis. Either could produce very similar symptoms, but I'm pretty sure it is cholera. In which case, I'm required to notify it under international health regulations.'

'He's lost a lot of fluids.'

'Yes, we'd better deal with that straight away.' Kate accepted the proffered large needle. 'Into the femoral vein. There we go.' She smiled reassuringly at the man. 'He'll need to be admitted, obviously. Let's get some fluids run in as fast as possible until his pulse and BP are back to normal.'

'You want a fluid input—output check?'

'Yes, please. It could take several days to get his levels back to what they should be. We'll start him on one a day cotrimoxazole as well. Let me know if there's any marked deterioration in his condition.'

It was almost noon before Kate was finally able to make her way back to her room, where she swallowed a refreshing glass of fruit juice and headed, yet again, for the shower. Twenty minutes later, dressed in white cotton trousers and a lemon-coloured T-shirt, she reached for her bag and hurried across the compound.

She told herself that it was excitement at the prospect of seeing something new and nothing at all to do with the way Sam's gaze lingered appreciatively on her slender figure that made her heart miss a beat as she climbed into the passenger seat.

'Where exactly are we heading?'

His mouth twisted as he saw the tell-tale tide of colour wash into her cheeks. 'North, to one of the larger villages. I was out there about six months ago, trying to persuade them to let me vaccinate the children against measles.'

'With no luck, I take it?' Kate hung on as they set off.

Sam frowned, flapping his hand at a hovering fly. 'There's often an inbuilt resistance—suspicion, if you like. I'm hoping the prospect of a threatened epidemic will make them more responsive.'

She turned her head to look at him. 'And if it doesn't?'

He didn't answer immediately; he needed all his concentration to keep the truck on the pot-holed road. 'I'm counting on one certainty.' He glanced briefly in her direction.

'The Masai prize their cattle, but they adore their children. I have to persuade them that the threat is very real. That's one reason I want you with me. If I get the go-ahead, we strike while the iron's hot. There might not be a second chance. We vaccinate the lot— adults too.'

'Sounds as if we could be in for a busy afternoon.'

He grinned. 'Wishing you hadn't come?'

Wishing she knew the *other* reason why he had wanted her to be here!

Smiling, she took off her hat, wiping her hand across the back of her neck before turning to lean against the open window. In the distance a darkening bank of cloud hovered against the horizon but rain was still a tantalising illusion as they drove through some of the most breathtaking scenery Kate had ever seen.

'Those are Kikuyu farmlands.' Sam followed the direction of her gaze.

'What kind of crops do they grow?'

'Mostly tea and coffee. Look at the soil. It's almost blood-red.' He leaned across her to point into the distance. 'The Great Rift Valley.'

Kate drew in a deep breath. 'It's beautiful.'

'What you're seeing is one tiny glimpse of it. Those hills around it can reach as high as twelve hundred metres and the floor is studded with volcanoes.' One hand retained a firm hold on the wheel as he directed her gaze. 'There's the Menengai and the Suswa. There are several others. The names are all Masai words.'

He broke off, swearing softly as he changed gear to negotiate a deep rut in the track. 'We should reach the *enkang* in about fifteen minutes.'

'*Enkang?*'

'It's the Masai name for a settlement.'

They began to descend deeper into the valley, passing gazelles, wildebeest and zebra. They skirted a busy Masai trading town before heading up again into the hills and turning onto a rough, dirt track, passing herds of cattle.

'This is everything I dreamed Africa would be,' Kate breathed as Sam finally brought the truck to a halt.

He followed her gaze, smiling, as he switched off the engine. 'Africa isn't all poverty and death and disease. I'm not saying they're not still a fact of life, but there's so much more—so much promise. You just have to keep telling yourself that one day it will all be like this.'

'It's going to take a long time, Sam.' She climbed slowly out of the vehicle to stand beside him.

'True. It won't happen in my lifetime. At least we have to believe that what we do now will make it easier for the next generation.'

He reached for one of the insulated boxes, handing it to her. 'Guard this with your life. It's the vaccines. I'll bring the vitamins and orange juice and the other bag. We'll set up in the shade under those trees. Oh, and by the way, don't be surprised if someone spits on your head, hands or feet.' He grinned at her look of horror. 'It's a form of greeting by some of the more elderly Masai. They don't grip hands—they just touch palms as a form of greeting. Kissing is strictly between women and women or women and children or brothers and sisters.'

She gave him an old-fashioned look. 'Thanks for the

warning. Is there anything else I should know? Some little item you might have forgotten to mention?'

He grinned. 'If I think of anything I'll be sure to let you know.'

'Oh, thanks, Sam.'

'Relax. Judging from the size of that queue, I think we'd better make a start, don't you?'

With a little help from a boisterous group of young-sters, they set up the tables and an awning in a small, wooded glade of acacia trees next to a small stream.

As she set out the tray of medications, Kate was aware of a young girl coming towards them. She couldn't have been more than about seventeen. She was tall and very slim and around her shaved head she wore a single string of beads. She wore a brightly coloured *kanga*, the patterned cloth worn by women throughout Kenya, and—in common with most of the Masai—the highly decorative beadwork in the form of earrings and necklaces. She smiled shyly. Kate smiled back, glanc-ing at Sam.

'Kate, this is Siwengi. She speaks some English so she'll help translate. Siwengi has been to school. She hopes to be a doctor one day. Siwengi, this is Dr Stewart.'

The girl grinned shyly, showing even, white teeth. 'Doctor.'

'I shall be glad of your help,' Kate told the girl, producing a spare white coat from her bag. 'Perhaps you'd like to slip this on and we can make a start.'

Siwengi's face broke into a beam of delight as she proudly donned the coat. 'I am ready, Doctor. We make a start, yes?'

'Good idea,' Kate smiled. 'Before that queue gets any longer.'

Within minutes she was seeing her first patient. Within the hour, seemingly indifferent to the noise going on around her, she had listened to chests, examined feet and checked ears, eyes and throats, pausing only to drink bottled water before turning to her next patient.

The man was sixty years old, tall and gangly and clearly unwell. He sat heavily on the chair provided, shivering as he held his *karasha*—the cotton cloak—around him.

Kate looked at Siwengi. 'Will you ask him what is wrong?' She waited as the girl translated.

'Meiyoki has the malaria.'

'Oh.' Kate looked slightly startled. Sam looked across at her, smiling as he shook his head.

'The Masai call any fever malaria,' he prompted softly. 'He might be right but don't take it for granted.'

She gave a rueful smile. 'Thanks for the warning.' She pushed a strand of hair from her eyes, studying the man carefully. His skin was dewed with sweat and he was wheezing breathlessly, clutching at his chest as he produced a dry, rasping cough.

Kate's face registered nothing of what was going through her mind as she spoke quietly to the man, uncoiling her stethoscope and persuading him gently to allow her to examine him.

Having listened to the rapid, shallow breathing, she dropped her stethoscope to check the rib movement, glancing at Siwengi. 'Will you ask him if he has any pain?'

The girl spoke to the man and looked at Kate. 'He says here.' She pointed to Meiyoki's side. 'Very bad when he breathes and when he coughs.'

'Yes, I'm not surprised.' Kate sat back and reached for the thermometer. 'And how long has he been like this?'

The man considered, then held up his hands.

'A week.' Frowning, Kate retrieved the thermometer and studied the reading. 'Yes, well, he certainly has a fever.' She hunted through the bottles set out on the tray. 'I think he has pleurisy. I'm going to give him some tablets.'

She shook a supply of antibiotics into a smaller bottle, handing it to the man. 'Tell him he must take one of these three times a day until they are all finished. And these—' she counted a supply of painkillers into another bottle '—will take the pain away. He should rest until the pain is better and the fever goes away.'

Watching the man shuffle away, supported by Siwengi, Kate glanced in Sam's direction as he completed a vaccination before handing the howling infant back to its mother.

'Having fun?' she teased lightly, nodding in the direction of the next, clearly unconvinced recipient for his attention. 'Got them lining up, I see.'

'Careful, woman,' Sam growled, 'or you could find yourself swapping jobs here.'

'No chance.' Quiet laughter gurgled in her throat as she smiled sweetly. 'You carry on being the villain of the piece. You're so good at it.'

'You'll be sorry,' came the softly murmured response.

She turned away, grinning, leaving him to laugh softly as, blushing furiously, she turned her attention to the next patient, smiling reassuringly as the woman lowered herself slowly into the seat.

There was no answering smile. The woman, who must have been about forty years old, was thin and listless. She sat with her eyes half-closed, occasionally lifting one hand to brush wearily at the hovering flies.

Gently persuading the woman to lie on a mat behind a canvas screen, Kate spoke quietly to Siwengi.

'Will you tell her I need to know where the pain is and how long it has been troubling her?'

Siwengi questioned the woman, listening carefully to the faintly spoken replies before looking at Kate. 'Nolmemeri has pain in her belly—not long.'

'Right, I see.' Kate spoke reassuringly to the woman as she made a thorough but gentle examination. It quickly became obvious that even the slightest pressure on her abdomen caused severe pain.

'Has she been vomiting?' Kate glanced at Siwengi. 'Ask her if she has any diarrhoea.'

Siwengi spoke to the woman again. 'She says some sickness, some diarrhoea.'

'Oh, great.'

'Problems?' Sam finished scrubbing his hands and came to smile at the woman.

'I'm not sure,' Kate said hesitantly. 'She's complaining of pain in her abdomen. I thought it might be appendicitis but. . .' She shook her head. 'The rest of the symptoms don't fit.'

'Want me to take a look?'

'I'd be grateful. I'd hate to miss something vital.' She moved aside so that he could move closer. 'There's been some vomiting, some diarrhoea.'

'Hmm, either of which could cover a multitude of sins.'

'Her general condition isn't too good.' Kate ran a hand through her hair. 'She's definitely underweight, lethargic.'

'Any rash?' Frowning, he leaned closer to examine the woman's skin. 'Ah, look here. This is interesting.'

Kate peered. 'What? I don't see. . . Oh.' She stared at the area of small blisters on the woman's feet. Frowning, she glanced at Sam. 'But I'm still not. . .'

'Dermatitis. We call it ground itch. Does she have a cough?' He spoke to the woman and nodded. 'She has a cough; sometimes she coughs up blood.'

Kate sat back on her haunches, staring at him. 'So, just what are we looking at here? It's not like anything I've seen before.'

He smiled. 'I haven't seen too many cases myself,

surprisingly enough. I'd say what we have here is a case of ancylostomiasis.'

She stared at him. 'Ancy. . .?'

He grinned. 'Hookworm.' His mouth tightened fractionally. 'It's a nasty little beast, one of the main causes of anaemia out here. Larvae penetrate the skin, hence the rash on her feet. They work their way around the system and into the lungs.'

Kate made a sound of disgust.

'The good news is that it's treatable. The bad news is that it's not so easy to change standards of personal hygiene and sanitation. I'd give her mebendazole twice daily for three days, or a single dose of pyrantel might be better. At least that way you know she'll actually get the medication and won't just feed it to the cattle or toss it away. Better treat the anaemia as well.'

'Thanks a lot.' Kate flashed him a look of gratitude.

'Think nothing of it.' He looked at his watch. 'All finished?'

'Yes, I think so.'

'Good, so have I. A good afternoon's work, I'd say. Hungry?'

'Don't!' Groaning, she eased her back. 'I was trying not to think about it. I skipped lunch and I'm starving.'

'Naughty, naughty, Dr Stewart.' Packing away the last of the equipment, he rose to his feet. 'Come on, let's go and eat.'

She stared at him. 'You're serious?'

'Absolutely.'

'What, you mean a picnic?'

'Even better.' His blue eyes glinted briefly.

'Sam. . .' She was on her feet, watching him warily. 'What are you up to?'

He grinned. 'I promise you, you'll enjoy it. Come on, take a look around while you're here.'

She held back. 'Won't they be offended? I mean, isn't it a bit like prying?'

He laughed. 'The Masai are sociable people.' They crossed the settlement together. 'This is a fairly large *enkang*. There are about a dozen houses.'

'Are they always built like this? With the cattle in the centre and houses around the enclosure?'

Sam followed her gaze. 'That's the Masai style.' He smiled as a young woman came to meet them. 'This is Kwosenga. She welcomes us to her house and asks that we eat with her and her family.'

Kate watched as a group of elders, swathed in their *karashas*, gathered around a small fire. 'Are there always so many people around? Surely they don't all live in the *enkang*?'

Sam smiled. 'No, we must have arrived in time for a special ceremony or celebration.'

'What are they drinking?'

'Honey beer.' He grinned. 'It looks harmless enough. Believe me, it can take the top of your head off.'

'Sam, I'm really not sure. . .'

They were joined by a tall Masai who smiled a greeting, showing even, white teeth. 'Dr Sam, it is good to see you again.' He extended a hand, lightly touching Sam's palms with his own.

'Leseamon, it is good to see you again. This is Dr Stewart, who works with us at the hospital. Kate, this is Leseamon, also known as Adam. His father is one of the elders,' Sam explained.

The two men spoke together.

'What is he saying?' Kate murmured.

'He welcomes us to his *enkang*. He asks how is my health? How is my family, how are my cattle and my goats? The Masai consider it impolite to rush into conversation without first having dispensed with the formalities.'

The tall Masai indicated a mat, inviting them to sit and, smiling, Kwosenga busied herself at the fire, sitting beside it on a low seat.

'What is she doing?' Kate whispered.

'Making tea.'

'Tea?' She gave a slight laugh. 'You mean, as in *cup* of tea?'

His mouth twisted. 'Tea is probably the most popular drink amongst the Masai.'

Kate watched, fascinated, as Kwosenga gently blew on the embers of the fire. Having brought them to a glow, she reached for a saucepan.

'Tea in a saucepan!'

'There's an art to the ceremony,' Sam murmured. 'It's always done this way.'

'I hope I'm going to like this, Sam.'

He grinned. 'Trust me.'

Kwosenga poured a cup of water into the saucepan, watching as it came to the boil. Next she reached for a handful of leaves, adding them to the water. Then she added milk, poured from a gourd.

'The gourds are cleaned with a long stick and ash from the fire,' Sam leaned towards Kate, speaking softly. 'You'll find it gives the tea a smoky taste.'

'I'm really pleased to know that, Sam.' She sat with her hands tucked around her knees as Kwosenga kept a watchful eye on the milk and just before it boiled tossed in a handful of sugar.

'The Masai are very fond of sugar. At the very least they use about four teaspoons per cup.'

Kate gave an involuntary gulp. The milk began to foam and rise in the saucepan and just as it reached boiling point Kwosenga gracefully leaned over to pick up the handleless pan with her bare hands, placing it gracefully on the floor.

Kate winced. 'How does she do that without burning herself?'

Sam's mouth twitched. 'It takes years of practice.'

Kwosenga poured tea into cups, handing them around. Kate accepted hers, sipping tentatively at the contents. To her surprise it tasted good and she drank appreciatively.

'Mmm, that's wonderful.'

Kwosenga smiled, saying something in her own language as she rose to her feet, smiling at Kate. Sam nodded.

'What is she saying?'

'She says it is good to welcome a new friend. Her husband, Leseamon, and his friends are preparing a special gift in your honour.'

'A gift? For me? Oh, but there's no need. . .'

Sam gave a slight laugh. 'It's the way the Masai do things. It's intended as a compliment.' He spoke to Kwosenga, who responded with shy laughter, before he moved to the door of the hut.

'Hey!' Kate was on her feet, scrambling after him. 'Wait for me. I'm coming with you. I'm supposed to be the guest of honour, don't forget.'

Sam's hand came down on her arm. 'I don't think you should, Kate. Wait here with Kwosenga.'

'Wait!' She flashed him a look of disbelief. 'You're not serious? I wouldn't miss this for the world.'

He frowned slightly. 'I'm really not sure this is a good idea. . .'

She laughed. 'You know your trouble, Sam Brady? Deep down you're just a good old-fashioned male chauvinist.'

His eyes glinted briefly as he studied her flushed cheeks. 'You're making a big mistake, Kate. Don't say I didn't warn you.'

'I won't,' she flung at him as she ducked her head to go ahead of him into the compound.

'I had a feeling you might say that,' he murmured.

CHAPTER TEN

LESEAMON and his brother-in-law, Morani—who was, if anything, even taller than Leseamon—were gathered with a group of the younger men around a small fire.

As Kate and Sam approached, Leseamon grinned, showing even, white teeth, and spoke to one of the teenage boys, who set off at a graceful lope for one of the huts.

Several of the women and girls had, by this time, come to join the group, laughing and chattering noisily. Several of the younger girls stared shyly at Kate, fingering her clothes and giggling, as she in turn admired their colourful beads and necklaces.

The younger women came clutching their babies, and instinctively Kate found herself reaching out and asking to be allowed to hold one in her arms. The mother said something in her own language as she gave Kate her baby, eyeing her shyly, and the other women laughed.

The fact that they were obviously enjoying a joke at her expense didn't bother her in the least—until she caught Sam's sardonic grin.

'What are they saying?'

'They're fascinated by the colour of your hair and eyes. They say we'll make many beautiful babies together and they hope they will all be like you.'

Scarlet-faced, she handed the infant back to its mother, conscious of Sam's dark gaze fixed on her as he controlled his laughter.

'Yes, well, I hope you put them right,' she flung at him.

'Why should I spoil their fun?' She caught the feral gleam in his eyes as he looked at her. 'I told them it was early days and that you were very shy.'

She felt the breath catch in her throat. Suddenly the thought of having Sam's children filled her with a kind of longing she had never thought possible. With a quick movement she turned away, but not before she'd heard him chuckle softly.

It was a relief to be distracted by the return of the teenage boy, leading a small goat at the end of a rope.

'Oh, look, isn't it gorgeous?' Laughing, she caught at Sam's arm. 'It must be the children's pet. They've brought him to show me.'

'The Masai don't keep animals as pets, Kate,' Sam put in quietly. 'Animals serve a purely functional purpose as far as they're concerned.'

Something in his tone made her glance up at him, her smile fading slightly. She brushed a strand of hair from her eyes. 'Yes, I suppose they would.' She looked at him again, smiling hesitantly as realisation began to dawn. 'Oh, lor, you don't think. . .? Sam, this isn't my gift?'

'I rather think it might be.' His mouth tightened and suddenly, confusingly, she was aware of his hand at her waist. 'Kate, I don't think this is what you imagine. It might be best if you. . .'

She didn't hear the rest. 'Shh, Sam, look.' She watched, fascinated, smiling as the young Masai covered the goat's mouth and nose with his hands. The goat seemed to stagger, falling to its knees, and her smile faded.

'But. . .' She glanced at Sam, saw the tension in his eyes and felt her heart miss a beat. 'I don't understand, Sam. What are they doing? Why. . .?'

His arm suddenly tightened around her. She could feel the muscles, taut against her warm skin. 'Kate, don't look. Look at *me*, my love.'

But it was too late. Even as she began to suspect what was going to happen, it was all over. A knife blade glinted in the sun and suddenly there was a bright gush of crimson as blood spilled onto the ground. The goat made a strange gurgling sound and within seconds it was being skinned and dismembered before her stunned gaze.

She knew that the colour had drained from her face. 'They killed it, Sam. They cut its throat.' She moistened her lips with her tongue, aware of Sam's arm drawing her close like a shield. She could feel the tension in his muscles. 'I'm going to be sick.' Her stomach heaved and she pressed a hand to her mouth.

'No, you're not,' he said quietly. 'It's over, Kate, all over. Take a few deep breaths and smile.'

Nausea washed over her in waves. She watched in dumb horror as what, seconds ago, had been a living, breathing animal became so many lumps of meat skewered onto sticks. *Smile!* She couldn't believe he had actually said it and yet, somehow, with an effort she did just that.

'Hold on, just a few minutes longer and I'll get you out of here.'

Vaguely she was aware of him saying something, his voice holding a note of teasing amusement. There was an answering ripple of laughter, then he patted her arm. 'On our way, darling.'

Darling! She must have imagined that bit, she told herself. Shock could do that—could have all sorts of strange effects. Her breathing was constricted as he drew her away from the smiling group, moving slowly with his arm round her.

It was all so smoothly managed that before she knew it they were back at the truck, the settlement behind them lost to view behind the trees.

'It's all right; you can relax now.'

She leaned against the truck, gulping hard and waiting for a wave of nausea to pass. 'I'm sorry,' she said faintly. 'I didn't handle that terribly well. It was a bit of a shock. I didn't expect. . .'

'It's over, Kate, forget it.' His thumb brushed against her cheek.

She shivered, treating him to a scathing look. 'I don't think it's going to be quite so easy.'

'Hey, come on,' he said quietly. 'I know it came as a shock. I did try to warn you.'

She sniffed. 'You knew what was going to happen, didn't you?'

'I had an idea.' His dark brows drew together. 'You have to remember the Masai have a vastly different culture to ours. What happened back there was our equivalent of being handed a sizable bouquet. The goat was sacrificed in your honour.'

'Poor goat. It was only a baby, Sam.' She felt the tears well up to sting at her lashes. 'I'd much rather have had a bunch of flowers.'

His lean fingers fastened gently on her arm to draw her roughly towards him, and when she would have pulled away his other hand came up to tilt her chin. 'Don't, Kate,' he rasped. As he looked into her eyes his hands tightened fractionally on her shoulders and he drew a harsh breath.

'I've been wanting to kiss you all day.' Then, when she offered no resistance, he caressed her flushed cheek, drawing her towards him and breathing against her hair as she relaxed against him with a sigh.

'You're right,' she murmured, loving the feeling of being in his arms. 'I overreacted.'

'Hey, you did what most people would have done.' He touched her cheek and the effect was devastating. She wondered if he was aware of it then, blushing, realised that he must be as his hand moved slowly to caress the curve of her breast, surprising the taut nipple as it flowered into a blatant signal of her desire.

'Kate,' he groaned softly as his mouth made marauding advances over her throat, lips and eyes and back to her mouth, claiming it with a fierce possession that left them both breathless. 'Oh, God, I want you. I want to make love to you, here and now.'

She drew a shuddering breath. Her senses felt drugged. She stiffened in his arms, saw the turmoil in his eyes and panicked as she sensed how little it would take to make her surrender.

He surveyed her in silence, his eyes narrowing on her pale face and then, with a ragged sigh, he reached out and drew her roughly towards him.

'I've been telling myself I wouldn't let this happen,' he rasped, 'but it seems I only have to be near you to lose control.'

Kate swayed slightly as his mouth hovered a breath away. What was she doing? Hadn't he just said that this shouldn't be happening? He bent his head to brush a kiss against her faintly protesting lips. Her breath snagged in her throat, the slight shift of her body closing the infinitesimal distance between them. She heard the soft intake of his breath before his mouth descended on hers as a hawk swooped on its unsuspecting prey, except that she was certainly no victim.

She could feel the powerful strength of his hands through the thin fabric of her blouse. An involuntary shiver of desire ran through her.

Sam was instantly aware of it. 'Don't be afraid,' he murmured. 'Let it happen, Kate. You know it's right.'

How could she deny it when she wanted him with every fibre of her being, especially when his hands were moving over her body, rousing her again? She closed her eyes, moaning softly.

'This is crazy, Sam.'

'Don't fight it.' His voice roughened. 'Do you have any idea what you're doing to me?'

'I'm not sure I do,' she murmured as her fingers traced the sensuous mouth. 'I never seem to be able to think straight when I'm with you.'

Sam groaned. 'I need you to be part of my life. I can't let you go—you do know that?'

She raised herself to reach his mouth. 'I want you too—I thought that must be obvious—' She broke off with a moan as he kissed her again.

'Shall I stop? I'd better warn you that I'm not sure I can.' His fingers had long since dealt with the buttons of her shirt and she gasped as his fingers caressed the soft swell of her breasts. Desire licked like a flame through her senses, sending dangerous signals to her brain.

She swayed, her body hungry with suppressed emotions which had lain dormant for too long. 'I've never felt this way before,' she whispered, feeling his warm breath against her hair.

'But you want me?'

'Yes,' she sighed huskily. What was the point of denying it when her own body was betraying her? But what about Sara? The thought set a tiny alarm bell ringing in her brain. She thrust it away as quickly as it arose. If this was all there was she would settle for it.

He raised his head to stare at her with glittering eyes.

'Trust me, Kate.'

She wanted to—desperately.

A nerve pulsed in his jaw, then he drew her slowly towards him. She could feel the need that was pulsing through her body like molten liquid. His hands moved to her shoulders, to her hair. She moaned softly, her own breathing laboured. Her arms went round his neck.

'I want you too, Sam,' she said huskily. She felt him tense. She said hoarsely, 'That doesn't mean I want or *need* a commitment. . .' Her voice trailed away on the lie. She wanted Sam—*all* of him for the rest of her life—but if that wasn't possible. . . She swallowed hard. 'I'll settle for what we have right now, Sam.'

She saw his face tauten with some undefined emotion

as he held her from him. He was breathing hard as he stroked her hair. 'I won't hurt you—you know that?'

'Yes,' she whispered. 'I want you to make love to me, Sam.'

His mouth came down to take possession of hers again. It wasn't a gentle kiss—it was fierce and demanding, marauding her senses until she moaned for release in the only way possible.

'I don't intend rushing things,' he said huskily. 'God knows, I want you—right here and now.' He drew a harsh breath as he looked at her for a long moment, then he put her gently from him. 'Not here,' he rasped. 'When I make love to you I want it to be perfect. I want to explore every secret, beautiful part of you.' Her body tensed as he drew her closer. 'Let's get back. Later we'll have all the time in the world, my love.'

They arrived back at Ramindi an hour later. For the most part they had driven in silence.

Cutting the engine at last, Sam seemed loath to move. Reaching over, he tilted her chin and looked into her eyes. 'I don't know how I'm going to carry on as if nothing has happened.'

She grinned. 'I know the feeling.'

'I think perhaps I'd better kiss you again, just to keep me going,' he said gravely, before his lips came down tenderly on hers.

Moments later, breathlessly, they broke apart. Sam climbed out, reaching for the bags. 'I have to do a round. Will you be all right?'

She nodded, feeling the colour surge into her cheeks. 'I think I might just go and take a very cold shower.' Reaching for her own bag, she half turned away, only to feel his hand on her arm.

'Kate, no regrets?'

'No,' she turned to look at him. 'No regrets.' Not

now, anyway. Maybe later, when it all had to end. But she wouldn't think about that.

As they walked across the compound together she glanced up at him and saw him grinning.

'What are you laughing at?' she flung at him, unable to prevent her own, totally illogical laughter from breaking out.

'I was just remembering the look on your face when you saw what happened to the goat.'

'That wasn't funny, Sam.'

'No,' he agreed gravely, 'it wasn't. But when I made our excuses to leave I had to give a reason for our rather sudden departure. You were, after all, the guest of honour.'

She stopped in her tracks. 'Yes, I've been wondering about that.' She flung him an accusing look. 'Just what did you tell them, Sam Brady?'

His mouth twitched. 'Well, since they obviously thought you were my woman anyway I thought I might as well play along with the idea. I told them you were in a somewhat delicate state of health.' His hand reached out to gently caress her stomach.

Her eyes widened as realisation dawned. 'Sam Brady, you didn't!'

They were still laughing as they walked up the steps and Sam pushed open the door. Then Kate glanced up and felt the colour drain from her cheeks.

Sitting in the office with a cup of coffee in his hand, a smile on his face and looking, for all the world, perfectly at home, was Jeremy.

CHAPTER ELEVEN

KATE came to a halt, her laughter fading and the shock of recognition leaving her limbs frozen and stiff, as Jeremy rose unhurriedly to his feet.

His gaze narrowed briefly as he seemed to study the two of them and then, in a couple of easy strides, he had crossed the room to take her in his arms.

'Kate, darling!' He slid an arm round her waist and Sam's dark eyes followed the movement. 'It's been a long time, but worth every second of the waiting just to see you again.' Jeremy drew her towards him, kissing her soundly.

'Jeremy. . .I don't understand,' she managed at last as he finally and reluctantly set her free. 'What on earth are you doing here at Ramindi?'

His attractive features assumed a slightly pained expression. 'I wanted to see you, of course, my darling.' His mouth twisted in the boyish way she remembered so well.

She brushed a hand weakly against her forehead, telling herself that this couldn't be happening. 'Yes, but. . .how? Why?'

Her confusion seemed to amuse him. 'I'm working for the World Refuge agency at one of the camps about fifty kilometres from here.' His voice took on a slightly humouring note.

He looked, she thought, just as Jeremy always looked—even despite the heat—tall, cool and good-looking in a clean-cut sort of way. She stared at him, searching desperately for something to say. It was ironic that so often during the past months she had imagined this moment; had known exactly how she would deal

149

with it, yet now that it had arrived shock seemed to have left her tongue-tied.

She was vaguely aware of Sam, standing in the doorway, his face taut and all trace of laughter gone. She swallowed hard. 'I. . .I'm sorry, I haven't introduced you. Dr Sam Brady. Sam, Dr Jeremy Carter.'

Beside her she was aware of Jeremy stiffening. 'Brady.'

Sam's dark head moved in brief acknowledgement, his expression unreadable. She sensed that he was angry without quite knowing how, yet when he spoke his voice remained calm.

'What brings you to Ramindi? We're a little off the beaten track for casual visiting.'

'Not exactly casual.' Jeremy reached out to grasp Kate's hand, his thumb brushing against her fingers. 'Kate and I are old friends—very good friends.' He smiled at her. 'We'd often talked about coming out to Africa together. I knew she was at Ramindi so when a patient needed to be brought to the hospital obviously I leapt at the chance.' He smiled down at her.

'I've thought about you a lot. We have so much catching up to do, don't we, darling? It will be good to talk about old times.'

She stared at him, telling herself that this couldn't be happening. What could they possibly have to say that hadn't already been said? He had made his choice; he had chosen Anna and she had wished them both well. Maybe not sincerely—not then. She had needed time and space. Coming to Africa had given her that, Africa and Sam. . .

With an effort she managed to keep her voice even. 'This has all come as a bit of a surprise, Jeremy.' She looked at her watch. 'Look, I'm sorry, I'm due on the ward; I have to do a round. . .' Swallowing hard, she looked at Sam. 'I'll be with you in about five minutes.'

'It's all right; I can cover. Take all the time you need.

As Carter said, I'm sure you both have lots to talk about.' Then, with a taut nod, he was gone before she could say another word, and she was left staring blankly at the door as it closed behind him.

She was scarcely aware of anything as Jeremy's voice continued in her ear. She closed her eyes in a feeble and totally unsuccessful attempt to shut Sam, at least temporarily, out of her thoughts. Her nerves suddenly seemed to have become an emotional battlefield, with the enemy on both sides and nowhere to run.

'Alone at last.' Jeremy's hand tightened over hers as he smiled down at her. 'I realise this has probably come as a bit of a shock and it isn't the ideal time or place, Kate. But later. . .there are so many things we need to talk about.' His hand smoothed hers, and he gave her the full benefit of the boyish smile. 'You do know how pleased I am to see you again?'

She cut him off. 'Jeremy, why are you here?' she demanded, knowing that she was still shaking from the shock of seeing him again. 'I mean, why are you really here?'

'I told you—I had to bring a patient in for possible surgery. Abdominal pain, drop in blood pressure, unexplained vaginal bleeding. All the signs of an ectopic pregnancy. . .'

'That isn't what I mean and you know it.' She managed to evade him as he pulled her towards him again. 'I meant why *here*, why Africa? Why *now*?'

He released her with obvious reluctance, his mouth tightening sullenly. 'I don't blame you for being annoyed. I realise it's a shock. I should have warned you but everything happened so quickly, and we really do need to talk, Kate. I realise now I've been such a fool.'

She shook her head, feeling a sense of panic beginning to overwhelm her. Swallowing hard, she managed to say lightly, 'I think we said everything there was to say a long time ago, Jeremy.'

He dismissed that, ignoring her protest as he drew her closer and brushing a hand against her cheek. 'You don't really believe that,' he said, gruffly. 'I know we can't forget what happened but we were both too emotional.'

She almost laughed aloud. It seemed, looking back on it, that *she* had been the emotional one, Kate thought. *She* had been the one whose world had fallen apart, while Jeremy had remained calm.

She ran a distracted hand through her hair. 'Jeremy, this isn't fair. I don't know what you want from me. You made your choice—you chose Anna.'

'I know what I did, what I said, and I'm not proud of myself. But things are never quite that simple, are they? Maybe we were both a little naïve, but people can change, Kate. Situations can change.'

She felt her heart contract painfully, as if she were being dragged into a void. 'Jeremy, this is all past. I don't see the point in re-opening old wounds.'

'At least you admit there are wounds.' His hands were on her shoulders, forcing her to look at him when she would have turned away. 'I accept that I hurt you.' He raised her face between his hands, kissing her before he released her slowly.

'I know we can't talk right now, but there are things I have to say to you, Kate. Things I need to say.' And then, as if sensing her resistance, 'I've come a long way to try to put things right between us. I'm sure I *can* put them right if only you'll hear me out. Don't you at least owe me that?'

She almost gasped at his arrogant assumption that she owed him anything. 'Jeremy, I'm sorry, but I really do have a round to do. . .'

'Kate.' His lips brushed against hers. It was a gentle kiss, undemanding, nothing earth-shattering. Safe, completely safe. And then, as if he sensed her weakening, 'For old times' sake, if nothing else. Can't we just spend some time together, talk as friends, before I have to leave? Is it so much to ask?'

Was it? It's because I'm tired, she thought, surrendering her mouth to his but feeling none of the stirring of her emotions his kiss would once have aroused. It was over. She almost laughed aloud at the thought. Finished. So what had she to lose? 'I'm not sure, Jeremy. . .'

'There must be somewhere in this God-forsaken place where we can find a little privacy?'

She stared at him unhappily. 'I suppose there's always the staff recreation room, but. . .'

'Go and do your round. I can keep myself occupied.' He kissed her again, lightly, on the mouth. 'I'll be waiting for you.'

She found herself battling against a feeling of resentment. She wanted to call him back; to tell him that he couldn't just walk back into her life like this and pick up the pieces as if nothing had happened. But he was already striding away and she could only watch as the door closed behind him.

With an effort she pulled herself together and made her way across to the ward. It was a relief, for once, to discover that things were relatively quiet. She had certainly never been more glad of the solid routine which, if it didn't keep her mind fully occupied, at least kept her hands busy.

'Any new admissions?'

Smiling, Jill made a final entry in the report book before handing it over. 'All quiet so far, touch wood.'

Kate scanned the report, flipping the pages. 'How's Mr Warungu?'

'His BP is up slightly.'

'Well at least that's an improvement.' Kate frowned.

'I'll take a look at him while I'm here, just to be on the safe side.'

Standing at the bedside, her fingers automatically reached for Daniel Warungu's wrist, feeling the pulse beating gently beneath her fingers. She smiled at the man. 'Well, that seems a little better, too. A couple of days and the co-trimoxazole should make a real difference.' She glanced at Jill as they moved away. 'Keep pushing the fluids—that's most important.'

'Will do.'

They made steady progress along the ward together, finally reaching the small office. Concentrating on the notes she was writing, Kate glanced at her watch. 'I don't suppose you've seen Sam?'

'Mmm,' Jill frowned, 'about an hour ago. He went through here with a face like thunder. Why, did you want him?'

It had to be the understatement of the year, Kate thought, shivering slightly as tiredness and reaction set in. Right now what she wanted more than anything in the world was to put the clock back; to be in his arms. 'No,' she shook her head, 'it wasn't important.'

Without even being aware of it, she sighed. Jill glanced at her, a look of concern in her eyes.

'Are you all right?'

'What?' Kate brushed a hand across her eyes. 'Oh, yes, I'm fine. A ghost must have walked over my grave, that's all.'

Jill looked at the duty list. 'I gather we had a suspected ectopic pregnancy brought in. Sam's probably in Theatre. Do you want me to give him a message?'

Tell him I love him, Kate thought. What must he be thinking? How could she explain in a message that Jeremy no longer had a place in her heart—or her life? On the other hand, maybe it was for the best that she speak to Jeremy first before she tried to explain to Sam. She shook her head.

'No, thanks.' With an effort she managed a smile. 'I'll catch up with him later.' She blinked hard on a sudden and totally illogical misting of tears. 'Look, there's someone I have to see. Can you cover here for a while?'

'Yes, of course I can.' Jill stacked a new supply of dressings on the shelves. 'And if I see Sam I'll tell him you're looking for him.'

Jeremy was reading a magazine when finally she made her way to the recreation room. Putting it aside, he rose to his feet, smiling the familiar, boyish smile as she went towards him.

She was still wearing her white coat as if, in some small way, the symbol of her professionalism might help to reinforce the barrier between them.

If he was aware of it Jeremy gave no indication, however, as he took her in his arms, kissing her cheek before releasing her to hold her at arm's length.

'You've lost weight.'

'It's the heat,' she gave a slight laugh, 'and probably the diet.'

'Whatever it is, you still manage to look good. But, then,' he murmured huskily, 'you always did, Kate, my darling Kate.'

Drawing herself up, she moved away, defensively brushing a strand of hair from her eyes. 'Would you like coffee?'

'Only if you insist,' he said gruffly.

'It's not obligatory,' she smiled slightly, 'but I'm going to have some anyway.' Anything to keep her hands occupied. She handed him a cup. 'Shall we take it out onto the veranda? It's cooler out there.'

He followed her, took the cup from her hands, discarding it with his own, and came to take her in his arms. 'So tell me what you're really doing here, in a place like this.'

She frowned. 'I would have thought that was pretty obvious, Jeremy, I'm working.'

'You could do that anywhere,' he said lightly. 'You didn't have to come to a hell-hole like Ramindi.'

'It might have escaped your notice—' she was immediately on the defensive '—but this particular hell-hole, as you put it, happens to need good doctors.'

'I'm not saying it doesn't. I just happen to feel your talents are being wasted here, that's all.'

She looked at him steadily. 'I seem to remember you once told me I hadn't got what it takes to get to the top in a competitive environment,' she told him sharply. 'What was it you said? Oh, yes, I wasn't ruthless enough. I was too soft. I think those were your exact words.'

His mouth tightened sullenly. 'Come on, darling, you must know I didn't mean it quite like that.'

She tried to evade him, studying him more closely as he pulled her towards him, and found herself wondering how she could ever have considered him attractive. Good-looking, yes. But there was a sullenness about him now that she had never noticed before. He was like a small child who had had his favourite toy snatched away.

She stared at him and felt her heart contract painfully, wondering what exactly it was that she had ever seen in him. It was odd now to think that she could even have contemplated marrying him, could have suffered a whole gamut of emotions—from grief to self-reproach—until Sam had come striding into her life, turning it upside down and teaching her what love was really all about.

'Didn't you, Jeremy? So, how did you mean it? How should I have taken it?'

Suddenly he seemed angry. He released her abruptly, moving steadily to the decanter and glasses which stood on a tray. 'Damn the coffee—I need a real drink.' He motioned with the bottle in her direction. She shook her head, watching as he poured himself a generous measure of brandy.

'You always were too emotional, Kate. That's your trouble.'

Her head jerked up. 'I cared for my patients. Are you saying that was wrong?'

'No, I'm not saying that.' Jeremy stared into his glass, discarded it and came to put his hands on her shoulders. 'Look, I'm not handling this very well, am I?'

'Jeremy, I'm still not really sure why you're here. I mean, why join World Refuge. . .?'

He looked at her. 'You must remember, darling, we talked a lot about coming out to Africa together.'

'Yes, but that was before. . .'

His voice was soft now. 'I've had a lot of time to think over the past few months.' His thumb grazed her finger. 'The truth is. . . I've missed you, Kate. No,' he cut her off as she tried to speak, 'hear me out. It's more than that. I realise now that I made a bad mistake when I let you go.'

She stared at him, flinching as his grasp on her arms tightened. 'I'm sorry, I don't understand. I don't want. . .'

'It's simple enough, Kate. I should never have let you go. I was crazy; not thinking straight. But that's all over now.'

She tried to free herself. 'Jeremy, what are you saying?'

His mouth twisted. 'All right, if that's how you want to play it, I'm admitting I was a fool. What we had was good. . .'

Breathing hard, she wrenched herself free to face him. 'You threw away what we had, Jeremy. In any case, aren't you forgetting something? What about Anna? Doesn't she figure somewhere in all of this? As

I recall, you married her. Or have you conveniently forgotten?'

His mouth tightened. 'I don't blame you for what you're thinking. But you're wrong.'

She frowned. 'This isn't making sense.'

'Anna and I. . .' He reached for her hands. 'We aren't married, Kate. I think we both knew it wasn't working out.' The boyish grin was there again. 'How could it when it was you I really loved?'

Kate shook her head. 'I don't want to hear this. You made your choice.'

'But don't you see, my darling? I'm admitting I was wrong. I made a mistake. I should never have let you go.'

The smile would once have melted her heart, but no longer.

'Jeremy. . .'

'Surely we can talk things through? You've no idea of the kind of misery I've been through these past months without you.'

She gave a sharp laugh of disbelief. Had he any idea of what *she* had gone through? Had he cared? 'Talk to Anna nicely. Maybe you can patch things up.' She saw the faint colour rise in his neck.

'I can't do that.'

'Of course you can.' Impatience was subdued with an effort beneath a smile. 'Things have just got a little out of hand, that's all. Surely you didn't have to do anything quite so drastic as to leave St Maud's, just because of a tiff? Weren't you in line for the senior reg's job? Oh, come on, Jeremy,' she said briskly. 'Tell them you've had a chance to think things through and ask to withdraw your resignation.'

'I can't.' The colour deepened in his neck. 'It's too late. Someone else got the job.'

'Oh.' She stifled a feeling of impatience. 'Well, I'm sorry. You were in with such a good chance, too.' She felt a genuine flicker of sympathy. If nothing else, Jeremy had always been ambitious. She glanced at him. 'Just out of interest, who got the job?'

He seemed to be having difficulty swallowing. He muttered something vague under his breath.

'I'm sorry?'

He cleared his throat. 'I said Anna got it.'

'Anna!' She stared at him and gave a hoot of laughter as realisation dawned. 'Anna is the new senior registrar? So that's it! Your pride is hurt. You lost out to Anna. I'll bet you made her life hell in the process and when, finally, she had the sense to see you for what you are you thought you'd turn tail and come running back to me. You really are incredible, Jeremy, you know that?'

His face suffused with colour. 'Kate, you don't understand. . .'

She gave a sharp laugh. 'Oh, I think I understand perfectly. For once in your life things didn't go exactly as you'd planned, did they, Jeremy? You lost out. Well, strange as it may seem, I happen to like Anna. I also happen to respect her professionally. She's a damn good doctor.'

'Of course she is.' The words 'for a woman' hung, unsaid, in the air. Tight-lipped, he reached for the remains of his drink, draining it. There was an edge to his voice when he spoke. 'You've changed, Kate. You're harder.'

'I had to grow up.' She felt her anger die away, to be replaced by pity. 'Maybe you should try it, Jeremy. You're a good doctor when you're not too busy thinking about what's in it for you.'

He stared down at his glass. 'There's nothing wrong with ambition.'

'I'm not saying there is.' Her voice cooled. 'Only that you can't go through life stepping on other people and expect to get away with it.'

He looked at her for a long moment. 'So you're

not prepared to give it. . .us. . .another chance?'

'Sorry, Jeremy.' She shook her head, suddenly glad
of the growing darkness which hid the tears glistening
on her lashes. She'd taken a chance on what he had
cared to call love. If nothing else, it had taught her to
recognise the real thing when it came along. She thought
of Sam, waiting, and felt a tremor of desire run
through her.

'There's someone else, isn't there?'

She pulled a wry face. 'There could be.' If she hadn't
wasted too much time. 'Go back to Anna, Jeremy. She'll
be good for you. It would never have worked out
between us.'

'I still think you're wrong.' He discarded his glass
and drew her towards him. 'I could still make you
change your mind. I could change. Just say yes, Kate.
That's all it takes. I could convince you, my darling.'
And, when she stiffened in his arms, 'Can't we at least
still be friends? Is that too much to ask?'

Before she knew what was happening his mouth came
down on hers, his kiss silencing her cry of protest. She
thought briefly about fighting him and decided against
it. Whatever she had once felt for Jeremy no longer
existed. She almost wanted to laugh because, in a way,
his coming here had been the final catalyst she had
needed. He had finally, once and for all, set her free.

For a few seconds, almost with a sigh of relief, she
allowed herself to relax, pretending that it was Sam
who held her and Sam who was kissing her. Her mouth
trembled hungrily. She sensed Jeremy's momentary
hesitation before he released her, breathing hard.

'Marry me, Kate. Think about it. We could make a
fresh start. . .' He broke off, his gaze suddenly concentrated on something behind her.

She turned her head and became instantly aware
of the figure standing in the doorway, the mockery
in his eyes turning to contempt as he took in her

flushed cheeks and the glazed look in her eyes.

She struggled to free herself from Jeremy's embrace, feeling sick and conscious only of Sam's stony expression. It was all too obvious that he had drawn his own conclusions.

'Forgive me.' His voice was icy. 'I seem to have intruded at the wrong moment.'

'Sam, I. . .'

His taut gaze settled on Jeremy. 'I just wanted to confirm your diagnosis, Carter. The patient is suffering from an ectopic pregnancy. She's going up to Theatre shortly. Obviously if you feel you wish to stay then you must do so.' His voice was icy. 'I'm sure Dr Stewart will be only too happy to look after you. Now, if you'll excuse me. . .'

Her mouth opened to protest, to explain, but it was too late. Sam had already turned and was striding away.

'Sam, wait. . .'

'Kate, darling. . .'

She whirled round. 'Jeremy, go home. Go back to Anna. Just. . .go away. There's nothing for you here.' She was vaguely aware of the shocked expression on his face before she headed for the door.

Sam was in the office by the time she caught up with him, breathing hard. She pushed open the door and felt her heart hammering against her ribs as she forced herself to look at him directly.

'Sam, we have to talk. At least let me explain. It isn't what you think.'

His expression darkened. 'I don't need your explanations, Dr Stewart. You certainly don't know what I'm thinking. I doubt you ever could.'

Kate stared at him disbelievingly as he walked to the door. 'Sam, I love you—you have to believe that. Nothing has changed.'

He gave a short laugh. 'No, you're right, and perhaps we can at least be grateful for that. In the cold light of day we might both have had regrets. Better we found out before it was too late.'

Kate stared at him, her blue eyes wide with distress. What did he mean, they might both have had regrets? How could she possibly regret anything that happened between them? Or was he speaking for himself?

'Sam, I give you my word, you have no reason to be angry. . .'

His expression darkened. 'You must have loved him once. Sooner or later you might find yourself wishing it was him and not me.' He put her away from him, his breathing uneven.

'But it won't, Sam.' Her hand caught at his arm. 'Don't you see I love you?'

His hands tightened on her arms, putting her away from him. 'I'm not prepared to take that chance. There's a plane due out of Nairobi at the end of the week. I want you to be on it. Goodbye, Kate. I hope you'll be happy.'

But how could she be happy ever again without Sam as part of her life?

CHAPTER TWELVE

SOMEHOW Kate got through the next few days. She threw herself into her work in a haze of pain and confusion, wanting only to be gone—to have it end.

She saw Sam only fleetingly, and it almost hurt more than if she hadn't seen him at all. When their paths did cross he was courteous and aloof, the look of cool disdain in his eyes dashing any hopes she might have had that, somehow, they could put things right.

A few days from now she would be back in England. The thought filled her with despair as she worked, blindly carrying out her duties, glad only when darkness fell and she could climb into bed, exhausted, but frustratingly unable to sleep.

An ominous bank of gathering storm clouds had built up in the dawn sky as she made her way down the steps but the air was, if anything, even heavier—even more draining.

She shivered momentarily as she stood drinking in the breathtaking beauty of the new day as if, by so doing, she could imprint its magic for ever on her brain.

A faint mist hung over the ground. Within half an hour, she knew, it would have cleared, despite the tantalising rumble of distant thunder, and the heat would be as relentless as ever.

In the compound Greg was working under the bonnet of the supply truck, helped by one of the boys. He looked up, smiling, as she approached.

'Trouble?'

He wiped his hands on an oil-stained cloth. 'Hopefully nothing too serious. I thought yesterday something didn't sound right. We have to check. The last thing we need is a vehicle out of action.'

'Do you need it today?'

'It looks like it. We've had word of a suspected epidemic of some sort at Mkuru, about thirty kilometres from here. It could be a false alarm, but Sam's going out to check.' He slammed the bonnet down and looked at his watch. 'I'd better let him know it's fixed. He'll want to get the gear stowed and get started as soon as possible.'

'It's not measles, is it?'

He frowned. 'Not likely. We carried out a pretty full vaccination programme. Still, best be prepared for anything.'

With an effort she managed a smile. 'It's time I was heading that way too. There's still a lot to get through before. . .' She broke off, swallowing hard, and a look of concern briefly tightened Greg's face.

'Are you all right?'

She nodded, lowering her head to blink hard on the tears that suddenly welled up. 'Yes, I'm fine.' She drew a deep breath. 'I'm just beginning to realise how much I'm going to miss all of this, that's all.'

His mouth tightened. 'Look, I'm sorry. I heard you're leaving.' He brushed the back of his hand against his brow, leaving a smear of oil. 'If it's any consolation, we'll all be sorry to see you go. Sam's a bloody fool.' He looked at her, smiling slightly. 'There's still a chance he'll calm down. Whatever it is, he'll get over it.'

'I don't think so.' She gave a wry smile. 'Anyway, maybe it's for the best. I knew when I came here that my contract was only short term.' She matched her steps to his as they crossed the compound, digging her hands into her pockets. 'The sooner I start looking for something more permanent the better—for everyone's sake.'

'So what will you do?'

She shrugged. 'I don't know. General practice,

maybe.' Somehow the thought made her feel even more depressed and the sight of Sam's angry frown, as she made her way into the office, did nothing to relieve the tension.

A voice came, distortedly, over the radio and she felt a quiver of alarm.

'The weather's closing in, Sam. The rains could start any time. I hate asking you to come.'

'Don't worry about it.' Sam was packing equipment into boxes, his face grim. 'It sounds as if we could be talking about cholera. We need to be sure—to start treating it as soon as possible. How many cases?'

'Six, so far.'

'Right. I'll be with you in about. . .' he glanced at his watch '. . .two hours.'

'Watch yourself, Sam. The weather can turn nasty in seconds and I've heard there's a gang of poachers still in the area. They're a nasty bunch from all accounts.'

'I'll be OK. I'm on my way. Over and out.'

He rose and for the first time seemed to become aware of her presence. 'I take it you heard? I have to go over to one of the camps.'

Kate nodded. 'You said it could be cholera. Is there anything I can do to help? It sounds bad.'

'It is if it's cholera, and Steve Baxter isn't given to hysterics. Can you check that the truck is ready and make sure my rifle is in it?'

She felt the colour drain from her face. 'It is. I saw Greg. He's just finished checking it over.' Her mouth felt dry. 'Sam, you're going to need some help. If this turns out to be a full-scale epidemic you're not going to be able to handle it alone.'

'Can you think of any alternative?'

She stared at him. His tone was cool, unrecognisable as that of the man who had held her in his arms only a matter of days ago, and unconsciously she flinched.

'No, I suppose not.'

'Then don't waste my time. People could be dying.'

She stepped back, fighting a sense of frustration and helplessness as he thrust medications and dressings into his bag.

'Where's Jill?'

'Taking a clinic.'

'Damn!'

'For pity's sake, Sam, tell me what you need. Let me help. I am capable, you know?' Frustration drove the power back into her voice and for a moment he stopped what he was doing to look at her.

'I didn't doubt that you were, but this is scarcely the time to debate it.' He reached for his bag, snapping the locks. 'I'm taking a supply of co-trimoxazole. You could put some tetracycline in as well, just as a back-up.'

She obeyed blindly, taking boxes from the cupboards and packing them into the emergency kit. She pushed it towards him but didn't release it.

'Please, Sam, let me come with you. . .I can help.'

He took the bag from her lifeless fingers. 'Don't be a fool. You don't seriously imagine I'd even consider it?'

Her mouth opened but her voice seemed to be trapped somewhere in her throat.

'Why not?' Her voice shook with anger. 'You'd take Jill.'

His mouth tightened. 'Probably. But, then, it's hardly the same thing, is it? In fact, it's not the same thing at all.'

He turned and strode out, leaving her stunned and shaking, and she was still shaking later as she dealt with a gathering line of patients waiting to be seen.

For the next two hours she dealt with everything from a case of anaemia to septic wounds and a baby with an advanced ear infection.

It was mid-afternoon before she had seen the last patient and Julie Lyongi finally began to dispose of the used instruments and soiled dressings.

'I can finish here. Why don't you go and take a shower; try to relax?' she suggested, smiling.

'I think we've both earned a break,' Kate agreed, trying to ignore a throbbing headache. 'I wonder how Sam's getting on?'

'He'll be fine.'

'But what if it *is* cholera?'

'Sam will know what to do. We've dealt with it before.'

But I wanted to be here to help, the thought rose to torment her. She suppressed a shiver. 'What if he comes up against the poachers?'

Julie looked at her. 'The chances aren't very likely. They're more likely to keep off the beaten track. They must know they've been spotted.'

Quickly Kate gathered up the case notes. 'I'll take these over to the office and check if there have been any messages while I'm over there.'

She was on her way up the steps into the office when she heard the radio crackle into life. Dropping the notes onto the desk, she hurried to answer it, feeling her heart give an extra thud as she did so.

'Hello, Ramindi. Can you hear me? Come in, Sam.' The heavily accented voice came through the static, and with a sense of shock she realised that it wasn't Sam.

Her hand shook as she flipped the control button. 'Yes, I hear you. Go ahead. This is Ramindi.'

'Thank God. Look, I need to talk to Sam. Is he there? It's pretty urgent. This is Joe Peterson.'

'No, I'm sorry. Sam's out on another call. I don't know when he's due back.'

'Hell! I need to get hold of him fast.'

'He should be calling in some time soon. Have you tried the other stations? He was heading out to Mkuru.'

'Mkuru? I heard they've had some trouble with poachers out that way.'

Kate's fingers tightened involuntarily on the receiver. 'Yes, we had a call from Steve Baxter. You say you can't raise Sam?'

'There's a lot of static. The weather's blowing up. Maybe his radio is out.'

Kate swallowed hard. 'He's overdue calling in.'

There was a brief silence. 'Sam knows what he's doing. He'll be in touch.'

If it's possible, the thought hammered its way into her brain. It was only as the voice came more urgently over the radio that she realised she had been standing stock-still and that she was trembling.

'Ramindi, are you still there?'

She blinked hard. 'Yes, I hear you.'

'Look, I've got an injured stockman out here. He's in a pretty bad way. Is Greg there?'

'He's in Theatre.' She shook her head helplessly. 'He's not going to be free for at least a couple of hours.'

'Dammit! I can't wait that long.'

'Mr Peterson, can you tell me what's wrong?' She reacted instinctively to the note of tension in the man's voice. 'I'm a doctor. I may be able to help.'

'It's a head injury. He was thrown from his horse and hit his head. It looks pretty bad. He's lost a lot of blood. I'd bring him out to you but. . .'

'No, don't move him any more than you have to. Is he conscious?'

There was a moment's hesitation. 'No, he's still out cold.'

'But he is breathing?'

'Sure, he's breathing.'

'Can you describe to me how it sounds?'

There was another brief pause. 'It's sort of funny.'

'In what way funny? Do you mean fast, or deep and rasping?'

'Sure, that's it—deep and noisy. You're saying that's not good?'

Kate deliberately kept her voice even so as not to unduly alarm the man. 'It's difficult to say. It's possible he has concussion. I can't make a diagnosis without seeing him. There could be any number of possibilities.'

'Can you help him?'

'Yes.'

'Well, in that case, lady, you'd better tell me what to do in the meantime because he's not getting any better, that's for sure.'

Kate glanced at her watch. She had no way of knowing when Sam might be back. Head injuries were always an unknown quantity. At best, the man might be suffering from concussion. At worst, it could be something much more serious. He might even die unless something was done, and soon.

She spoke urgently into the receiver. 'Look, Mr Peterson. . .'

'The name's Joe.'

'Right, Joe, I'm coming out to you myself.'

'Look, girlie, that may not be such a good idea. The storm's about to break. It's already raining. . .'

'Joe, we don't have any choice. I'll get to you somehow. I'm not sure how long it will take. How do I find you?'

Static briefly drowned out his voice. 'Head due west. I'll send a man out to meet you.'

'I appreciate it. Meanwhile, if your man regains consciousness don't let him move around and don't feed him anything. Just keep him as quiet and still as possible until I get there.'

'I'll do that.' Seconds later he had signed off.

Kate hurried across the compound. She felt taut with apprehension as she sought out and explained the situation to Julie.

'Shouldn't you wait for Sam?' the girl said anxiously. 'He knows the area. He knows Joe Peterson.'

'I wish I could, but Sam may be away for hours yet.

I can't take the chance. From what Mr Peterson said it sounds urgent.' Kate shook her head. 'I'll be fine.' Reaching for a pack of sterile dressings, she glanced out of the window at the darkening sky. 'Let's just hope I get back before the storm hits.' She gave a slight laugh. 'I didn't think I'd ever hear myself hoping it wasn't going to rain.'

Julie handed her a supply of painkillers, her face anxious. 'I'll keep trying to reach Sam from this end. He won't be happy.'

No, Kate thought, grabbing the emergency first-aid kit, she didn't suppose he would. But right now she had no choice. A man's life was more important than the differences between them, real or imaginary.

She paused at the door. 'I'll be back as soon as possible. In the meantime, if you do locate Sam perhaps you'd better let him know what's happened. I'll keep in touch with you by radio here.'

Julie frowned. 'It might not be so easy to contact Sam. We've had trouble with the radio before. He has to leave the truck and the children climb all over it.'

'If it is children.' Kate met Julie's gaze. 'That gang of poachers is still around. I've seen what they can do. What if he meets up with them?' She didn't wait for an answer she didn't want to hear. 'I'll call you from the Peterson place to let you know what's happening.'

She set off in the truck at a pace which might have seemed sedate on a British country road, but which out here came close to recklessness.

She was an expert driver but the truck was heavy and, with a feeling of panic, she found it needed every ounce of her strength to keep it steady on the uneven ground.

She pushed a strand of hair from her eyes, feeling the film of perspiration dotting her skin. Taking one hand briefly from the wheel, she eased the thin white T-shirt from where it had stuck to her back. Even the breeze was hot—oppressively so—despite the distant rumble of thunder.

A herd of wildebeest grazed in the distance beneath the trees. Her gaze watched them warily, conscious of the fact that they were easy prey for a lurking leopard or some other hungry animal, waiting, hidden from sight, for the cool of the day when it would begin to hunt.

Her concentration wandered and she had to drag the wheel over hard as the truck hit a deep rut and juddered violently. Her foot rammed down hard on the brake and she came to a halt, leaning her head in her hands and breathing hard until her heart gradually resumed its normal pace.

Suddenly the vastness of the heat-seared wilderness hit her with such force that she began to shake. She felt vulnerable as she had never done with Sam beside her.

It was with intense relief that she heard the first heavy spots of rain, seeing them bounce against the windscreen. Laughing aloud, she stretched her hand out, relishing the warm moisture on her skin and closing her eyes as she pressed it to her face. At least she had been here to see the arrival of the rainy season.

When she opened her eyes again it was to see the other truck coming towards her and she raised her hand eagerly in response to the man's wave.

The Peterson place was large and rambling. They passed stables and outbuildings, a small office and a large, wooden bungalow, around which someone had attempted to create a garden.

A man came hurrying down the steps to greet her, standing in the rain to watch their approach. She guessed that Joe Peterson was about fifty-five. His face was tanned and, at this moment, his expression was anxious.

'You made good time.' They wasted no time on preamble. Kate followed him up the steps. 'He's through here. At least we managed to get him onto one of the beds.'

Brushing a hand through her hair, Kate was already opening the medical kit before she bent to look at the man on the bed. He was young—about thirty, she guessed—and he was still deeply unconscious.

She glanced up at Joe Peterson before she set quickly to work, pouring antiseptic into a dish and using it to swab away some of the blood. 'Has there been any change at all since I spoke to you?'

Joe Peterson ran a hand wearily through his greying beard. 'He came to for a few seconds, that's all.'

Kate felt a quick spasm of relief. 'Did he say anything? Did he recognise you?'

'He said, "Hello, boss. Bloody to-do," then he went out like a light again.'

Kate smiled slightly. 'Well, at least that's a good sign, Mr Peters.'

'Call me Joe.'

She glanced up, smiling. 'Has he been sick or complained of a headache?'

'Yes, sure, both. Is that good?'

Kate straightened up. 'I'd be more worried if he hadn't regained consciousness by now.'

'Does that mean he's going to be all right?'

She started as a flash of lightning briefly lit up the sky. Rain was hammering against the wooden roof. The strength of this storm was unlike anything she had ever seen or heard before and she found it vaguely frightening.

She frowned, forcing herself to concentrate. 'I'd like to be able to say he's not in any danger. The trouble with head injuries is that you can never be sure, especially without the proper equipment to monitor him. For now I'd say the odds are slightly in his favour.'

Her fingers felt for the injured man's pulse. It was shallow but reassuringly even. Swabbed clean, she was able to examine the wound on his temple more closely.

'It's not as deep as I'd feared,' she murmured, as much for her own reassurance as the man's beside her.

'Can you fix it?'

She nodded. 'It'll need stitching. I'll just check his neck first to make sure there's no more serious injury, then look at his eyes. That should give me a pretty good idea of whether there's any real damage.'

Very gently she moved the man's head from side to side. Then, using an ophthalmoscope, she spent several minutes looking for tell-tale signs of damage.

Minutes later she straightened up. 'Well, he's certainly severely concussed, but I'm happy to say I don't think there's going to be any lasting or permanent damage. It's just possible there might be a slight hairline fracture of the skull, but I'd say nothing worse than that.'

Joe Peterson drew a deep breath. 'He's going to be OK?'

Kate frowned. 'Concussion can be pretty nasty and, if there's any suspicion of a fracture, naturally I'd feel happier if we could get him to the hospital. But under the circumstances. . .' she glanced, frowning, at the windows, seeing the rain lashing against the glass '. . .I'd say the trip might do more harm than good.'

'So what can we do?'

'I'll leave some pain-killing tablets with you. When he does come round he's going to have one hefty headache. He'll probably be sick again too. He might complain of dizziness, even double vision. I want him kept as still and quiet as possible. He certainly shouldn't try getting out of bed for a while.'

'I'll see to it, Doc, don't you worry.'

She smiled, gathering up her equipment and snapping the locks on the emergency kit. 'The name is Kate.'

'Well, I'm grateful, Kate.'

'I'll fill out a report and let Sam have it. In the

meantime, if there's any change for the worse get straight on to Ramindi.' She followed him out of the bedroom.

'You'll be needing a drink. You've earned it.' Without waiting for her reply, Joe crossed to a refrigerator and poured two beers, handing her one.

She drank greedily, relishing the cool liquid as she sat on one of the chairs round a well-scrubbed table.

Minutes later she rose to her feet, setting the glass down. 'I must get back.' She handed him a box of tablets. 'Give him one of these when he wakes up. Try not to worry; I'm sure he's going to be all right, but if you're worried you know where to find us.'

Joe accompanied her out to the steps. 'You go easy, now,' he frowned. 'Better steer clear of the river. The water rises pretty fast down there.' He watched as, ducking her head, she flung the emergency kit into the back of the vehicle and drove away, raising her hand once before she was out of sight.

Driving had been difficult before but now it was a nightmare. In the distance, every now and again, forked lightning filled the sky with an eerie glow.

Kate's hands strained against the steering-wheel, her knuckles white, as she struggled to prevent the truck from sliding in what, in an amazingly short period of time, had become a quagmire. Torrential rain smashing against the windscreen obliterated almost everything. Several times she was almost obliged to stop, but somehow managed to keep going. If only Sam was here, the thought rose tantalisingly in her mind.

With almost fiendish deliberation, the radio chose that precise moment to crackle into life and she almost laughed aloud with relief as Sam's voice came over the air waves, bringing him—temporarily, at least—a little closer.

'Hello, Kate, are you receiving me?'

Her hand reached shakily for the receiver. 'Sam?

Yes, I can hear you. Where are you?'

'Never mind where I am. What the hell do you think you're doing?' His voice came back at her, tinged with such hostility that instinctively she froze.

'I don't know what you mean. Didn't Julie explain? There was an emergency call from the Peterson place. One of his stockmen was hurt.'

'I know about the call. I spoke to Ramindi about half an hour ago. I've been trying to contact you ever since. What I want to know is why the hell you took it upon yourself to go out there? Have you any idea what you could run up against? You knew the weather was closing in.'

'There wasn't time to debate the issue, Sam,' she bit back at the anger in his tone. 'There was no other choice. Greg was in Theatre and we couldn't reach you. Someone had to go.'

'And so it had to be you.'

'There was no one else.' She thought she heard him swear softly under his breath. 'And, in case you've forgotten,' she retaliated, 'I do happen to be a doctor.'

He said something of which she was only half-aware as her attention was distracted by movement seen vaguely through the cascade of water hitting the windscreen.

'Hello, are you there?'

'What. . . Oh, yes.' Her knuckles tensed against the wheel as she peered through the windscreen into the growing darkness, struggling to keep the truck from sliding.

'I said, how was the patient?'

'He was thrown from his horse and gave himself a pretty nasty head wound. It needed stitching. He has a severe concussion but I'm pretty sure there was nothing more serious.'

'It sounds as if you did everything you could.' He sounded almost grudging. 'So, where are you now?'

It was a good question. 'I'm not sure.' She grunted as the truck swayed. 'On my way back to Ramindi. Visibility is bad and getting worse.' Her gaze flickered again and this time she felt the first prickle of real alarm.

She watched in horror as a tree came crashing down only feet ahead of the truck, to be instantly carried away by a torrent of rushing water.

'Dear God. . .' It was little more than a whisper, the words seemingly stuck in her throat by a sense of rising panic.

The radio crackled again insistently.

'What did you say? Damn this static.'

'Sam?'

'I can hear you, but you'll have to speak clearly.'

'The river. . .' Her voice suddenly sounded oddly disjointed. 'It's. . .it's closer than I thought. It's in full flood. Trees are coming down everywhere.'

For one terrifying moment she thought that he had gone as silence hung between them. Sweat trickled down her face, but for some reason she was shivering uncontrollably. 'Sam, can you hear me?' Her voice broke on a sob of fear and she almost laughed aloud with relief when he spoke again.

'Can you see the track?'

'No.' She heard his sharp intake of breath.

'You must have strayed off it somewhere. Can you get back?'

'No.' She had to swallow hard before she could go on. 'It's almost dark, Sam. What I took to be the track must have been part of the old river bed, but there's water everywhere.'

'My God, a flash flood.'

She barely caught the words as suddenly the truck shifted violently, throwing her sideways. Her foot jammed against the brake, bringing it slewing to a halt. She cut the engine and sat for a moment, feeling sick and hearing something grate ominously against the door. She gave a soft whimper of fear.

'Kate, for pity's sake, don't lose your nerve—not now.'

She realised he had been speaking to her all the time and she hadn't been aware of it. 'Tell me what's happening. What can you see?'

'Nothing,' she said flatly, staring with growing horror at the rapidly widening, fast-moving rush of water. 'I'm not sure.' She screamed involuntarily as another tree came crashing down, to be carried away by the swirling flood.

'Kate! Kate, get away from there—now.' Sam's voice was tense. 'The flood water is washing down from the hills. You're right in its path.'

'I can't, Sam. I can't move.'

'Yes, you can. I want you to start the engine and move *slowly*. Take it easy—no sudden movements. Ease your way out. I'll get to you as soon as I can.'

Her foot was already on the accelerator and she turned the wheel, trying desperately to manoeuvre the truck. She felt it sway and had to fight to keep it under control. The wheels spun but nothing happened. She wasn't moving.

'Sam, don't put yourself in danger. There's nothing you can do.'

'I'm already on my way.' His voice sounded amazingly, reassuringly calm.

She was almost ashamed of the pang of relief his words sent surging through her. 'But where are you?'

'Cutting across country towards you. The river must be just ahead of me.'

Her foot came down on the accelerator again. The truck lurched forward, jarring her, and stuck again. 'The water is rising, Sam.'

'I know. Just keep trying, my darling. For pity's sake, keep trying.'

She gave an involuntary sob. He had called her

darling. It had all been part of the panic, of course, she knew that. He had only been trying to offer her reassurance, but for some reason her heart was pounding crazily.

She juggled with the receiver, needing both hands to control the wheel as she tried yet again to ease the vehicle forward. For an instant she released her hold, brushing away the tears that were streaming down her face.

The pull of the water was stronger now. Maybe she could jump clear. Pushing open the door, she gasped as she realised how much higher the water level had risen. Within seconds her hair was soaked, plastered to her head.

'Sam, I can't move the truck. I'll have to try to get out.' She gasped as the whole vehicle seemed to tilt, flinging her sideways to land at an awkward angle against the door.

Sam's voice was taut. 'Just hold on, Kate. I can't be more than a few minutes away from you.'

'Sam, this is crazy; stay away. You can't help.' She scarcely recognised the hysterical scream as her own.

His own voice was suddenly, strangely cool. 'Sorry, Kate, it's too late. I'm on my way. Just save your breath and hold on, my love.'

Terror had robbed the whole nightmare scene of any reality. Her reactions were all purely instinctive now. In desperation she struggled to grip the wheel, pressed her foot hard on the accelerator and conscious that, with every second, the raging torrent was gaining on her.

For one heart-stopping moment the truck juddered and shifted. Water washed over her feet. A scream started in her throat but got no further. The truck swayed and then suddenly the whole world seemed to tilt. She was falling, drowning.

Somewhere, from far away, she heard Sam's voice, calling out urgently. She heard a grating sound, felt a sharp blow against her temple and then the water closed over her head.

Someone was bathing her face gently with water. It was deliciously cool and she moaned softly.

'Kate, for God's sake open your eyes. Tell me where you're hurt. Say something.'

She listened to the voice, angrily resenting its intrusion into her consciousness and even more so the hands which, though gentle, were probing areas of pain of which she was only slowly, miserably, becoming all too aware.

'Come on, now, that's right. Open your eyes, my darling.'

She tried to obey but her eyelids seemed heavy, as if she were waking from a drugged sleep. It needed an effort of will but she managed it, closing them again quickly as the light made her gasp.

She lay for several seconds, trying to shake off the fuzziness that seemed to be clouding her brain. Her head ached and her hand rose to probe the spot, only to find a cloth pressed over it and someone else's hand.

'Sam?' Memory returned and she began to tremble so violently that her teeth shook. 'The flood. . .we've got to get away. . .'

'Take it easy. You're safe. I've got you.'

Suddenly she was in his arms, sobbing as he held her close. 'Oh, Sam, I was so afraid. I thought. . .I thought I was going to die.'

As if in a dream she felt his lips brush against her hair then her face and, as if it was the most natural thing in the world, she clung to him, responding to the kiss which finally reached her mouth, possessing it with a desperation that she had never known could exist.

He broke away at last and for the first time she looked at him clearly. His face was ashen and grim as he stared down at her.

Dazed, but conscious at last that she was safe, she stared into the haggard face. 'What. . .what happened, Sam?'

A nerve pulsed in his throat. 'I thought. . .I heard you scream and then the radio went dead. For one crazy moment I thought I'd lost you. Dear God, if it had been true.'

She felt weak tears coursing down her cheeks. 'But how did you find me?'

'The truck had turned onto its side.' His voice faltered. 'By some miracle the lights stayed on. You must have hit your head. There wasn't time to think about whether it might be serious or not. The water was rising—I knew I had to get you out.'

She swallowed hard. 'I was so scared, Sam.'

'Don't, don't, my love.' His own breathing was ragged.

'I thought I'd lost you.'

'It's all right; everything is going to be all right.' His voice was soft, so gentle that she scarcely heard it above the dull drumming inside her head. 'You're safe—that's all that matters. I don't know how I would have borne it. . . You were damn lucky,' he said tightly, 'when I think what might have happened.'

'Don't, Sam,' she protested weakly.

He bent to brush a hand against her cheek. His voice faltered again. 'You need to get some rest. I've given you an injection. It should help you to sleep.'

'Sam. . .'

He shook his head. 'Sleep now.'

'We have to talk,' she protested.

'Later.' He caressed her cheek. 'There's plenty of time, my darling.'

But was there? she thought as her eyelids began to feel heavy and finally fluttered to a close.

* * *

It was daylight when she woke again. Her head still ached and she was beginning to discover bruises in places she hadn't even known she had until now.

She lay drifting in and out of an uneasy sleep, reluctant to face the dawning realisation that, in spite of everything, nothing had really changed.

Perhaps the blow on her head had made her confused, she thought. She certainly felt tired and giddy. That must account for the fact that nothing made sense, for the fact that for an instant she had believed Sam was going to say he loved her—was going to ask her to stay. But it wasn't true. She knew it couldn't be because in just a few hours from now she would be on a plane, heading out of his life for ever.

It occurred to her as she lay there that she should finish her packing. But she seemed to have been gripped by a feeling of lethargy.

It need a real effort of will to force herself to get out of bed and make it as far as the shower, where she was horrified to see the full extent of her bruising.

She managed with difficulty to struggle into a sleeveless denim dress, and purposely left her hair loose.

A single glance in the mirror showed her a face that looked pale and drained, and there were dark shadows beneath her eyes. She was carefully applying a hint of colour to her lips, in an attempt at damage limitation, when Jill tapped at the door and came in.

'Hi, I wasn't sure you'd be awake yet. I came to see how you are.' She surveyed the bruises and winced. 'I'm not sure I should have asked. You really had a narrow escape, didn't you? Should you be out of bed yet?'

Kate gave a slight laugh. 'I'm not sure which is the lesser of the two evils. Now that I'm upright—' she winced as she moved '—I think I prefer to stay that way.' More seriously, she said, 'How's Sam?'

'Quiet.'

Kate flicked her a glance. 'But he's all right? I mean. . .' It hadn't occurred to her until then that he might have been hurt too, and her heart gave a sudden lurch.

'He's fine,' Jill offered the smiling reassurance.

'What about the epidemic? Was it. . .?'

Jill nodded. 'Cholera, unfortunately. But at least it's being dealt with promptly. Sam has arranged for the most severe cases to be transferred to Ramindi. Talking of which. . .' she glanced at her watch '. . .I'd better get back. I'll pop in to see you later. Oh, and strict instructions from Sam—you're to take things easy. Everything is under control, so lie around and be lazy if you feel like it.'

'It sounds a nice idea,' Kate said quietly, 'but I still have some packing to do.' She gave a slight smile, wincing as she reached for a neatly folded pile of undies, dropping them onto the bed. 'I knew I should have done it sooner. I just hadn't quite counted on this happening.'

Jill stared at her. 'But. . . Surely you're not still planning to leave? I mean. . . Why, for heaven's sake? Whatever it was between you and Sam, things must have changed.'

'I'd like to think so,' Kate said quietly. 'But that has to be Sam's decision. He hasn't asked me to stay. As far as he's concerned, nothing has changed.'

'Oh, come on. He will. Give him time.'

'Unfortunately that's the one thing I don't have.' Kate smiled crookedly. 'Maybe there are things we both need to work out. We've both made mistakes.' She swallowed hard on the tightness in her throat. 'Meeting Sam was something I hadn't counted on. I'd been hurt in the past, but so had he.'

Jill looked at her. 'You're in love with him, aren't you?'

Kate gave a shaky laugh. 'There's going to be one

huge, gaping hole in my life without him, that's for sure.'

'Oh, Jeez, Kate, can't you do something—*anything*? You can't just walk away. There aren't too many Sams around in this world. Believe me, I should know.'

Kate blew her nose hard. 'I don't really have any choice, do I? It takes two to make a commitment and I don't think Sam is ready.' With an effort, she pulled herself together. 'Don't worry about it. I'm just feeling sorry for myself. I'll get over it. There are other jobs, other places.' But not another Sam. She forced a smile. 'You'd better get back, and I have some packing to do.'

Jill's mouth tightened. 'I shall miss you.'

'I shall miss you too.'

There was no easy way to end a part of your life.

Her head was throbbing again. Rummaging in her bag, she found a couple of aspirins, swallowing them with a cup of strong coffee. Usually they would have made a difference. This time they didn't. Aspirin couldn't deal with the kind of pain she was suffering right now. She needed Sam; loved him more desperately than she had ever loved anyone in her life. She had thought he loved her too. But, she realised now, maybe love wasn't enough. There had to be trust as well. Without it there was nothing, and the sooner she accepted that the better.

She emptied a drawer, folding the items neatly into her suitcase which lay open on the bed. Finding a new job wouldn't be too difficult. Her father had often hinted that he'd be only too glad to have her join the practice yet, suddenly, she wasn't sure that she could face going back and picking up the pieces more or less where she had left off. Her life, so far, had seemed to consist of false starts. First Jeremy, and now Sam.

Her eyes misted with tears. She brushed them away fiercely. There had to be somewhere where she could get away from the memories—make a completely fresh start.

She took a dress from its hanger in the wardrobe and was folding it into the suitcase when the door was flung open.

Startled, she looked up, her face taut with strain, to see Sam standing in the doorway. His lips were set in a hard, fierce line.

'What the hell is going on? What are you doing?'

Her own breathing was suddenly ragged. It needed all her will-power to continue what she was doing. Collecting the few remaining toiletries from her bedside cabinet, she dropped them into a bag which she added to the suitcase. 'What does it look like, Sam? I'm getting the last of my things together.'

'You're packing!'

She glanced around the small room, spotted a pair of shoes and added them to the rest of her belongings. 'I'm afraid I left it a bit late but I'll be ready in plenty of time, don't worry.' Taking several deep breaths, she half turned away, only to feel Sam's hands on her shoulders preventing her from doing so.

He looked round the room as if bewildered. 'You're leaving. But I thought. . . Kate, what's wrong?'

She couldn't believe that he was asking the question. 'Wrong? Nothing's wrong. Why should anything be wrong?' She met his gaze with a level stare, almost afraid to believe what she thought she saw there. She broke away, glancing at her watch. 'The supply plane will be here in about an hour. I'm sorry, Sam, but I still have to finish. . .'

She broke off, flinching visibly as his grip tightened on her bruised arms. For a second, as if becoming aware of it, he relented, relaxing his grasp, but he didn't let her go.

He looked haggard, she realised. His face was pale. 'Kate, stop this.'

She looked at him. 'I'm sorry?'

He drew a rasping breath. 'I can't let you go.'

His face was gaunt as she stared up at him, biting at her lips to still their trembling.

'I. . .I don't understand. What are you saying, Sam?'

'I can't let you go,' he repeated. His own breathing was ragged as he held her, his hand gently cupping her chin and forcing her to look right into his compelling blue eyes. 'I'm asking you to stay, Kate.'

She looked at him, afraid to believe. 'But you said. . .'

He stared at her, his throat working. 'I know what I said. I've had time to think. I've come to realise a few things in the past few hours,' his voice rasped, 'not least that I almost lost you. Don't go, Kate. Please, don't go.'

Her eyes misted with tears as she stared up at him then, with a sob, she went into the safe refuge of his arms.

'Oh, Sam, I thought I'd lost you too. I was so afraid.'

'You could have been killed.' His voice was muffled as he held her close. 'When I found you, I thought. . .'

'Don't!' Her fingers brushed against his mouth, silencing the words and then, before she knew what was happening, his mouth came down on hers—relentless, firm, demanding.

They clung together, Kate offering no resistance as his hands moved with infinite gentleness over her body. He raised his head briefly to look at her. 'I need you, Kate,' he groaned softly as his mouth made feathery advances over her throat, chin, eyes and back to her mouth again.

She responded with an ardour that matched his own. She could feel the heat of his body through the thin T-shirt he was wearing and she was filled with a need to be part of him.

He swore softly as the fabric of her dress seemed to create a barrier between them until he finally dealt with the buttons and made contact with the warm silkiness of her skin. 'I love you, Kate,' he rasped.

'I love you too,' she said brokenly, her hands against his chest as she eased herself gently away from him. She closed her eyes briefly. 'There are things we need to talk about, Sam; things you have to know.'

'There's no need.' His breathing was ragged as he looked down at her.

'But there is, Sam. I don't ever want there to be doubts between us.' She held him off when he would have drawn her closer again. 'I thought I loved Jeremy, but that was a long time ago, and I was wrong.'

'I know.'

'My feelings for him could never compare with what I feel for you. What you saw. . .' She broke off, her eyes widening. 'You *know*? But you said. . .'

'I overreacted,' he rasped. 'When I saw you with him I had to hit out. I hated myself when I saw the look in your eyes, but I'd been hurt once and I couldn't bear the thought that it might happen again.'

'Oh, Sam,' She brushed her fingers against his mouth. 'Couldn't you have trusted me?'

'I did trust you. I do. When I'd had time to think about it I knew I was blaming you for what Sara did.'

She stared at him, wanting to believe him, but fear gave an edge to her voice. 'I'd never hurt you, Sam— you have to believe that.'

'I know,' he said roughly. 'But I wasn't only afraid for myself. Don't you see, if there was even the remotest possibility that your feelings for him weren't over. . .?'

'Sam, it was only after I met you that I realised what love, *real* love is. What I felt for Jeremy was. . .was infatuation. Worse than that, he was a habit I'd drifted into. Yes, I felt devastated when he met someone else, but I realise now that it was my pride that was hurt.' She looked at him. 'What I feel for you is something totally different. When I was out there alone, I wanted you, Sam—only you.'

'You could have been killed.' His voice was muffled as he held her close. 'Oh, Kate, my Kate. How could I ever have imagined I could let you go? If you had died out there, I would have wanted to die too.'

They clung together. He raised his head briefly to look down at her. 'I need you,' he groaned. 'I've been such a fool. I don't deserve you.'

She laughed gently. 'We've both been fools, Sam. Maybe we deserve each other.'

His glittering gaze narrowed as he drew her towards him. 'Does this mean you're prepared to take another chance?'

She took his face in her hands, kissing him gently. 'I love you, Sam.'

He bent his head to brush his lips against hers and looked at her, his eyes glowing. 'I love you too, my Kate.' He drew her roughly towards him and kissed her until they broke apart breathlessly, and he looked at her with laughter in his eyes. 'I suppose this means I'd better make sure there aren't any goats on the menu at the wedding reception.'

She hit him playfully. 'As long as there's me and you, Sam, that's all that matters.' And she reached up to kiss him again.

MILLS & BOON®

Medical Romance™

COMING NEXT MONTH

IF YOU NEED ME... by Caroline Anderson

Audley Memorial Hospital

Joe, now an Obs & Gynae consultant, had been fostered by Thea's parents so when, years later, she turned up on his doorstep, homeless and eight months pregnant, naturally he took her in. But behaving like a brother was difficult....

A SURGEON TO TRUST by Janet Ferguson

Anna's ex-husband had been a womaniser, and much as she liked working with surgeon Simon, she found it very hard to trust him, particularly when appearances suggested he might be just the same kind of man.

VALENTINE'S HUSBAND by Josie Metcalfe

Valentine dreaded her birthday, for it was her wedding anniversary too, a stark reminder of her husband and child, lost in a car accident. Escorting an old lady to France was the perfect escape, until she met Guy, a Casualty doctor, *and* Madame's grandson!

WINGS OF PASSION by Meredith Webber

Flying Doctors

After losing Nick, socialite Allysha had turned her life around and become a pilot for the RFDS, confident of her skills, but with no social life—until, quite unexpectedly, Nick arrived to replace Matt. How was she to convince him the change was real and lasting?

Available from WH Smith, John Menzies, Volume One, Forbuoys, Martins, Woolworths, Tesco, Asda, Safeway and other paperback stockists.

MILLS & BOON®

Four remarkable family reunions,
Four fabulous new romances—

Happy
Mother's Day

Don't miss our exciting Mother's Day Gift Pack
celebrating the joys of motherhood with love, laughter
and lots of surprises.

SECOND-TIME BRIDE   Lynne Graham
INSTANT FATHER   Lucy Gordon
A NATURAL MOTHER   Cathy Williams
YESTERDAY'S BRIDE   Alison Kelly

Special Promotional Price of £6.30—
4 books for the price of 3

Available: February 1997

MILLS & BOON®

Medical Romance™

Flying Doctors

Don't miss this exciting new mini-series from popular
Medical Romance author, Meredith Webber.

**Set in the heat of the Australian outback,
the Flying Doctor mini-series experiences
the thrills, drama and romance of life
on a flying doctor station.**

Look out for:

Wings of Passion by Meredith Webber
in February '97

*Available from WH Smith, John Menzies, Volume One, Forbuoys, Martins, Woolworths, Tesco,
Asda, Safeway and other paperback stockists.*

FREE!

FOUR FREE
specially selected
Medical Romance™ novels
<u>PLUS</u> a Mystery Gift
when you return this card...

Return this coupon and we'll send you 4 Medical Romance novels and a mystery gift absolutely FREE! We'll even pay the postage and packing for you.

We're making you this offer to introduce you to the benefits of the Reader Service™– FREE home delivery of brand-new Medical Romance novels, at least a month before they are available in the shops, FREE gifts and a monthly Newsletter packed with information.

Accepting these FREE books and gift places you under no obligation to buy, you may cancel at any time, even after receiving just your free shipment. Simply complete the coupon below and send it to:

MILLS & BOON READER SERVICE, FREEPOST, CROYDON, SURREY, CR9 3WZ.

No stamp needed

Yes, please send me 4 free Medical Romance novels and a mystery gift. I understand that unless you hear from me, I will receive 4 superb new titles every month for just £2.10* each, postage and packing free. I am under no obligation to purchase any books and I may cancel or suspend my subscription at any time, but the free books and gift will be mine to keep in any case. (I am over 18 years of age)

M7XE

Ms/Mrs/Miss/Mr _____

Address _____

_____

_____ Postcode _____

Offer closes 31st July 1997. We reserve the right to refuse an application. *Prices and terms subject to change without notice. Offer only valid in UK and Ireland and is not available to current subscribers to this series. **Readers in Ireland please write to: P.O. Box 4546, Dublin 24.** Overseas readers please write for details.

You may be mailed with offers from other reputable companies as a result of this application. Please tick box if you would prefer not to receive such offers. ☐

MILLS & BOON®

Enchanted™

We are proud to announce our
bouncing baby miniseries—

Each month we'll bring you your very own bundle of
joy—a delightful romance by one of your favourite
authors.

This exciting series is all about the true labour of
love—parenthood and how to survive it! Because, as
our heroines are about to discover, two's company
and three (or four...or five) is a family!

Look out in February 1997 for the Enchanted title:

The Bride, The Baby and The Best Man
by Liz Fielding

*Available from WH Smith, John Menzies, Volume One, Forbuoys, Martins, Woolworths,
Tesco, Asda, Safeway and other paperback stockists.*